HOT
ANIMAL
Love

ALSO BY SCOTT BRADFIELD

HOT ANIMAL

Love

Tales *of* Modern Romance

SCOTT BRADFIELD

CARROLL & GRAF PUBLISHERS
NEW YORK

Hot Animal Love
Tales of Modern Romance

Carroll & Graf Publishers
An Imprint of Avalon Publishing Group Inc.
245 West 17th Street, 11th Floor
New York, NY 10011

AVALON
publishing group incorporated

Library of Congress Cataloging-in-Publication Data is available.

ISBN: 0-7867-1576-6

Printed in the United States of America
Interior design by Maria Elias
Distributed by Publishers Group West

Jack Bradfield (1996–)
and Robert Bradfield (1926–)

different generations, similar stuff

Contents

Angry Duck

Mercy! What a speech—from what a bird!
—*Merrill,* The Changing Light at Sandover

Arnold Hingley — colleague

A. Of course I respected Sammy. But can't say I liked him much. I don't want this to sound prejudiced or anything, but he didn't fit in around here, if you know what I mean. And yet I was probably his closest friend in the department; we even shared an office. You wouldn't believe how messy and disorganized he could be. Especially that damn plastic wading pool of his, and the whiskey bottles and Jiffy Pop bags everywhere, maybe I shouldn't go into it. I'll just say Sammy did things his own way. Like he didn't know any other.

Q. What about his work?

A. Are you asking if I've read it?

Q.   (unintelligible)

A.   Yeah, I read it, maybe not that carefully or anything, it's not my kind of stuff. I'm more a Keats and Arnold sort of man—but don't print that, okay? It doesn't sound right, and I don't mean to disparage him. Because, okay, he wasn't easy to get along with, and maybe I'm not that big into contemporary poetry. But you had to respect his integrity. Sammy never compromised his vision. He always told the world exactly what he wanted to say.

Beverly Dunn — college teacher

A.   He just waddled into class one day. Last thing I expected. Wasn't enrolled, just waddled up from the local pond and straight into my Intro Poetry Workshop. He didn't understand the add/drop procedures, hadn't submitted any work for review, just came in and sat down like he belonged. He had this, oh, this swagger about him, right from the start. Of course it was defensive. He was terrified of being found out, pointed at, ridiculed. So he acted above it all, tough on the outside, like any true artist would. I can't tell you how many poets just never make it because, well. They don't have that toughness, that mean streak they need to carry them through. At the same time, nobody can write like Sammy without accessing some pretty deep emotional stuff. But despite that exterior toughness, he was an easy duck to hurt, my Sammy-boy. So when I heard about the world tour and how he wasn't coming back, I just. I mean . . .

Q.   Are you all right?

A. I'm fine, I mean, but.

Q. Should we take a break?

A. No, really. I was just saying that he was full of beauty, our Sammy. And brave in so many ways. The sort of student who walks into class and you know it right off. This is the real thing. This kid's a poet. It's important for a teacher, helping a student like that. It makes all the other, excuse me, all the other bullshit—the whining no-talents, the administrative hassles, the tenure battles—worth going through. Because you know a student like Sammy is waiting at the end of it. Waiting just for you.

Q. (unintelligible)

A. Of course I miss him. He's the best student I ever had. And he wasn't fully formed, either. He needed help and he appreciated it. He made me feel important for the first time in my life and I'll always miss that feeling. I'll always miss the best student I've ever had, and maybe my best relationship, in a funny way.

Aaron Cormier—fellow poet

A. A girl. It doesn't matter what species you are, right? It's always a girl.

Q. What was her name?

A. I don't know how much I can tell you. She started showing up for readings about the same time Sammy was developing his reputation in local coffee shops, always sat in the back, dressed to the max, totally in white except for that olive skin of hers, Catalan skin, but all the rest of her blond and dazzling with whiteness, you couldn't turn her off, man, you couldn't blot her out with a blackout curtain. White stilettos, short white skirts, white fishnet stockings, always too much and always too far away. She didn't pay any attention to the rest of us. She didn't even like poetry. She just came to the readings to be near him. And when he read, it was like he was reading for nobody in the world but her.

Q. What was their relationship like?

A. Their relationship was their relationship. What do I know? At first she would come and listen and, soon as it was over, she'd split. Afterward, Sammy'd go looking for her, but she'd be vanished, man, like into her own whiteness. And then, somewhere along the way, they just linked up, nobody knows how, and she was suddenly *always* around. Kind of like his Yoko. Whenever you saw Sammy, there she'd be. Sitting beside him and stroking his back.

Bunny Fairchild—agent

A. I heard about him from Beverly; she invited me out for the Eliot Awards. Sammy had won first place that year, already getting national coverage, and the best part? That kid knew how to handle a crowd. He'd waddle up to the mike with total self-control, huge with confidence, especially for a duck. This is me, his body language told you. I'm a fucking duck and so what? I can't remember what he read—I just remember the confidence, it was like something separate from Sammy, not part of who he really was at all. Always one eye on the crowd, never letting them off the hook, saying this is me and *this* is what I've come to say. The crowd loved him for it.

Q.   How soon did you take him on?

A.   I went home that night, made some calls, and had five figures by morning. I know five figures doesn't sound like much, but in the world of poetry? We're talking space rocket, darling. And Sammy and I were riding it straight to the moon.

Arnold Hingley — colleague

A.   I always felt he brought the drinking with him. It was certainly a full-blown problem by the time he got here, all the usual clichés. Bottles in the filing cabinets, not showing for classes, shuffling down the hallways half sloshed in his bathrobe and slippers. We're pretty sure he was sleeping in the office; you wouldn't believe the mess I'd find some mornings. But people who knew him say it started with his first book, *The Angry Elegies*. Didn't know what he'd done or how to do it again. Sophomore blues. And, of course, you don't need to know much about Sammy's work to see it's all about anger. He had to let it out. For Sammy, that's what self-expression was for.

Q.   How was he with the students?

A.   Ask the students.

Q.   Would you have any names?

A.   I was acting associate head that year, and I heard complaints all day long, usual stuff about how their grades weren't high enough, teacher wasn't fair, and so on. But the complaints against Sammy, how should I put this . . .

Q.   How should you put it?

A.

Q.   Professor Hingley?

A.   I think I'll leave it at that.

Theresa O'Day — student

A.   He hit on me.

Q.   What do you mean "he hit on" you?

A.   What do you think I mean? He hit on me. He made improper advances like every chance he got. Kept trying to climb up on my lap, especially if I was wearing a skirt, swear to God. Kept asking me to scratch his tail feathers. *That* kind of hitting on me. You want me to draw a picture? I was like barely twenty years old and feeling really impressionable and he really, you know, like they say in the student handbook, he misused his disciplinary authority as mentor. So I filed a complaint with Professor Hingley, and know what he did? Blew me off. Getting hit on and getting blown off. That's what this stupid English Department is all about.

Q.   What about his teaching methods? How was he at communicating with the students?

A.   You're putting me on.

Q.

A.   Mainly he'd come to class totally sloshed, drinking something out of this chipped blue ceramic mug that said "Bawdy Bard" on it, smelled like rotgot gin, swear to God. He kept falling off his desk, flapping like crazy, feathers everywhere. Then he'd read this crappy poetry he was writing, something about the universe, and we were all bound up in the metaphor, he called it a philosophical prose-poem or something, it didn't make any sense at all. He kept referring to it as his "second book," but I heard he never wrote a second book. I heard he wrote the first book, got all famous and so forth, and that was it. Bye-bye, birdy.

Q. When was the last time you saw him?

A. When he gave me that fucking C and I came looking for him and I knew he was in his office, I could hear him snoring behind the door and I started pounding on the door, I didn't care who heard me, and shouting, "You gave me a fucking C! You make me scratch your fucking tailfeathers all semester and you gave me a fucking C?" And he didn't have the balls to answer the door, big surprise. I'm sorry, you know . . . I mean, what happened to him on that world tour, it was terrible and all. But I'm afraid I don't feel any compassion in my heart. That was one mean, selfish duck. And I don't care if his first book of poetry really *was* a big deal and all.

Aaron Cormier — friend and fellow poet

A. I'd like to read you something.

Q. Please.

A. It's one thing to sit around talking about Sammy, and dredging up his past, things he said and did and probably shouldn't've and so forth. But I want to read you something that's really about Sammy, probably the first thing I ever heard of his . . . here. The beginning of the "Pond Cycle" in the *Elegies*. I'm sure you know it.

Q.   Of course I know it.

A.   These days, everybody with a BA knows it. It goes like this:

> Fucking ducks—
> You fucking stupid fucking *fucking* ducks
> Swimming around
> And around in your fucking stupid, stupid
>   fucking smelly pondwater scum
> You stupid. Fucking. Ducks.
> Quack qauck quack quack quack quack quack
> quack (ad infinitum)
>   —quack.
>   Would you please just shut the fuck up.
>   SHUT UP!
>   SHUT UP!
>   **SHUT UP!!!**
> You fucking, fucking ducks.

Q.

A.   There's nothing to say about something like that, is there? Because it's poetry, man. It speaks for itself, and that's what Sammy was all about. Not the drinking and the gossipy bullshit you're looking for, or the failure that haunted him, or that tragic world tour. It's the poetry he had in his heart. Anger and beauty, more than anybody can bear. And he made a gift of it to all of us.

Q.   (unintelligible)

A.   Well, I'll just leave that to you and the talking heads at PBS to decide, won't I?

Alfred A. Bolger — editor

A.   No, I don't think we put too much pressure on him. I don't think we put any pressure on him at all. Only Sammy put any pressure on Sammy. Sure, we had good receipts on the first book, but there were also a lot of returns, so while we definitely intended to stick with Sammy over the long haul, how should I put this? We're committed to publishing good contemporary poetry here at Knopf. But at the same time, we're not actually champing at the bit to publish it in today's marketplace. It takes the wind out of your sails, commercially speaking.

Q.   Did he show you what he was working on?

A.   Yes, he did. You know, it's no secret, the second book's always a bitch, especially if you feel as passionate about your work as Sammy. And there was some good stuff in it—don't get me wrong. It was definitely ambitious. I'm not entirely certain, but I think basically what Sammy wanted to do was tackle the cosmic Blakean nature of being a, you know, a duck.

Q.   Would you have any early drafts?

A.   Well, maybe, but that wouldn't be fair to Sammy. He wasn't happy with it. The work was inconsistent and he knew it. And then the social stuff started getting in his way, the readings, the job at New England U., and he got increasingly involved with that, I probably shouldn't say this, but that succubus, the Lady in White. I can't remember her name.

Q.   Lola Montez.

A.   Yeah. You meet girls like her all the time on the poetry circuit. Olive skin. Depthless black eyes. Dressed entirely in white. Girl had legs up to her neck.

Q.   You didn't like her much.

A.

Q.   You were saying . . .

A.   How I felt about Lola never mattered. She was this natural force that picked Sammy up and put him down again and when she was finished it was suddenly too late. There was nothing anybody could do but sweep up the feathers and walk away.

Weirdo — fellow duck

Sammy sammy sammy. Quack quack quack quack quack. Sammy sammy quack quack quack, Mister Bigshot, Mister Bigshot. Quack quack quack quack. Crackers crackers crackers, gimme more crackers and I'll quack quack quack quack. Who reads poetry anyway quack quack quack. What's the big deal anyway quack quack quack quack. Where's Mister Bigshot now, that's what I ask you? Quack quack quack quack quack. Where's Mister Bigshot now?

Herr Doktor Hans Fischer — critic and academic

A.   *Ja*, we had the distinct pleasure of meeting Herr Sammy during his first European tour, and it was a great honor for him to visit our modest Book Fair in Erlangen. He spoke, I guess it was for several hours, on the importance of his work and his reasons for literary triumph in the mass market. However, I fear he may have been drinking too much Weissbier both previous to and concurrently with the discussion of his work, but it is not unusual to witness this form of behavior at a book fair, especially in Bavaria. We were very honored by his appearance, however, and impressed that he had flown so far to be with us. His lady friend was very charming also, though I can never remember her name quite correctly.

Q. Lola Montez.

A. I believe that is accurate. She was a very lovely girl all dressed in white, who did not speak too much to anybody other than Sammy, but you always knew she was present. I believe that Sammy was the first avian poet to have performed his readings in Erlangen, making him the subject of many interesting reviews and profiles in the German culture pages. Though, as I recall, Sammy did not like to be referred to as an avian poet, which he considered very derogatory. We sympathized with this viewpoint very much.

Q. It may have been his last public appearance.

A. I believe I have heard this also. He discoursed at length on the topic of being a poet in an age of commercial hypocrisy and expressed many interesting, though quite random, observations about human behavior, such as the eradication of the ozone layer, human hunting laws, the arrogance of NASA, and the fact that his poetry was not about being a duck, which to me was especially interesting. Instead, he said his poetry was about expressing the ineffable, I believe he was to characterize it as the cosmic animal dilemma of all creatures who aspire to Godhood. Though there were times, I must confess, when he was very confusing, perhaps it was my poor English-language skills. And when he fell off the podium and lost consciousness, we were unable to pursue these interesting topics any farther.

Q.   You say he read something.

A.   This is accurate. And I have taken the liberty to pre-
serve a page from his presentation. He described it
as a book he was working on concerning his
Blakean revision of totality. I am not a professional
reader, nor is my English very proficient, but I shall
enunciate as clearly as possible:

> quack quack quack quack quack steady-state
> theory quack quack quack quack quack teleolog-
> ical misprision quack quack quack quack not
> your anxiety of afflatulence Mister *Man* quack
> quack quack quack aspirational Godhood quack
> quack quack duck not I not duck quack quack
> quack quack quack apex of whiteness quack
> quack quack quack . . .

And so forth. It is not so easy to read, however,
for it has been written in red felt pen on the
back of this stained bar napkin, which is falling
to pieces, as you see. But it does provide an
indication of where he was going in his further
creative endeavors.

I, for one, look forward to a critical edition
of his final papers very much.

Aaron Cormier — friend and fellow poet

A.   We'll never know, will we? The only person who
will know is Lola, and she isn't exactly speaking
volumes.

Q.   When was the last time you saw her?

A. We held a memorial for Sammy at the Poetry Café,
    took turns reading from the *Elegies*, reminisced, got
    drunk. I'm pretty sure I saw her drive up outside—
    I mean, it must have been her. How many people in
    central Connecticut drive a palomino-white con-
    vertible BMW? She came up to the door and hesi-
    tated, but I didn't see her come in. Maybe she felt
    responsible for what happened in Thailand. Maybe
    some of us felt she was responsible, too.

Q. Do you think Sammy was self-destructive?

A. He was very self-destructive. That goes without
    saying. As a poet, he took the biggest step imagi-
    nable to produce his first book. He climbed up out
    of the pond and turned his back on everything he'd
    ever been and everybody he ever knew. There was
    only one place to go after that. Into the next book.
    Turning his back on any world that made him feel
    like he belonged. Success, New York, us, the world.
    For Sammy, poetry was always an act of expiation.
    It didn't surprise me when he let Lola book that
    tour of Asia and the Mideast. In a funny way, it
    didn't even surprise me what happened to him.

Arnold Hingley—colleague

A. Who can you blame but Sammy? Who told him to
    get drunk and go wandering alone through the
    streets of Singapore, even if he was carrying a copy
    of Rilke under his arm? Those people like their
    waterfowl. They're not going to invite you into their
    little streetside café and pump you full of Malaysian
    hooch to get you reading from your next book.

Beverly Dunn — teacher

A. This is the grade book I used for his first class, there he is. Sammy the Duck. He was never actually enrolled at the university; so I signed him in through Adult Ed. And here's one of his early poems; it was eventually revised as a concluding "outrage" in the *Elegies*. Oh, and look, a box of crackers I kept around for his tutorials. That was one thing about the pond Sammy never left behind. His passion for crackers and popcorn.

Lola Montez — friend

A. I don't have anything to say. Please go away.
Q. We just wanted to ask a few questions about Sammy.
A. I know what you want to ask me. Why can't you just let him rest in peace?
Q. People are interested in Sammy, Lola. Some are even interested in you.
A. You don't understand, do you. I don't want to talk about him. I just want you people to get out of here and leave me alone.

Beverly Dunn — teacher

A. Of course I remember the first thing he ever said to me. He waddled into class that day and took a seat, never once acted like he didn't totally belong, just muscled through the roughest sea, that was our

Sammy. And nobody said anything. I was taking roll, looking for his name on the list, the students all pretending not to notice, I didn't know what to say. And then I looked at him and we made eye contact, he was staring right at me, waiting for me to acknowledge his presence. And then I realized I didn't have to say anything. He was going to say something to me.

"Quack," he said. "Quack quack."

It was so Sammy. But then you'd have to have known him like I did to know exactly how Sammy it was.

Men and Women in Love

The first time Sandra Snyder left her boyfriend, he came after her in his truck. He took her mother's door off the hinges with a tire iron and they had it out right there on the front porch for the whole neighborhood to see. "You thingamabobbing sheesh-eating you-know-what," Sandra reenacted later for the benefit of her sister, Theresa. "And he's screaming, 'You bleeping sheesh-flitting flabber-jabber.' People are shouting out their windows; 'Shut up!' 'The baby's sleeping!' 'This is a family neighborhood, you whore!' Tony tries to throw me over his shoulder like a sack of laundry and I go for the rake, give him my best shot—*pow*, right in the kisser. I'm no longer some pretty little Barbie he can undress for bed. I'm a freethinking individual with my own thoughts and opinions. Which

17

is, of course, about the same time he lets me have it with the tire iron. And that's all she wrote."

They were trying out a new alfresco coffee bar at the indoor mall. Theresa had this thing lately for decaf cappuccinos.

"Let's try Sears later, okay?" Theresa tried not to appear too interested in Sandra's love life—it only encouraged her. "You just reminded me. Dan needs a new basket for the mower."

Sandra licked the last sugary drops from the inside of her styrofoam cup. Then slammed it down on the wobbly table with a fragile little *pock*.

"Next thing I know I'm awake on the couch, Tony weeping over me, telling me he loves me, baby, why do we keep doing this to each other, sweetheart? It was like, I don't know. Like being picked up by this mighty wave and being set down again. This big bang and roar and then, so gentle, a baby crying on my stomach, and a bag of ice dripping down the back of my neck. At first— *bang!* And then—*ahhhhhhh*. Like all that energy and bad feeling being let out of you. And me expiring in his arms like this gigantic lacy beautiful balloon."

A few weeks later Sandra returned home early from work and found Tony in bed with a Filipino girl who worked at the Laundromat.

"It's not what it looks like!" Tony shouted. When he came out of bed he wasn't wearing anything but his St. Christopher medallion. "It's complicated, honey. Let me try and explain."

Tony was never very good at thinking on his feet. Sandra, on the other hand, suddenly possessed a deep interior calmness, like blue water in a lonely grotto. The world slowed down a little. It gave her the time she needed to catch up.

Sandra looked in the bathroom and saw soaking towels on the floor. Then she tried the kitchen. She could still hear Tony shouting. He was pulling on his pants and stumbling into the hall.

"Don't jump to conclusions," he warned her. "You know what happens when you jump to conclusions."

The entire apartment was breathing around her like some billowy submarine creature. Don't rush, the walls told her. Don't go anywhere you don't want to go. Sandra opened one kitchen drawer, then another. Finally she selected a waffle iron from under the sink, and just as Tony came in she let him know what she'd decided. It was a simple, firm decision. He never knew what hit him.

The girl from the Laundromat started screaming, and Tony started bleeding. Then Tony got to his feet, grabbed Sandra by the hair, and dragged her into the living room. The girl from the Laundromat wouldn't stop screaming because she didn't understand. This wasn't about *her*. This was about *them*.

By the time Tony got to the fire tongs, everything was pretty inevitable, really. It was as if Sandra had been waiting for these particular fire tongs all day.

"I thought he'd kill me," Sandra told Theresa. They were sitting in their mother's kitchen drinking Instant. "I was so scared it was almost like elation. Like I'd lifted up out of my own body somehow, flying high above everything, beating my wings in the air and soaring. Then somehow the police showed up. The girl from the Laundromat, I don't know, someone opened the door. They went after Tony and I went after them. This wasn't *their* house, I told them. This was *my* house, all *mine*. What is this? I kept screaming. *Nineteen eighty-four?* Some kind of thought police? Then, before I knew it, I found the fire tongs in my hands, and I knew I had to show them. At which point, of course, one of them shot me. He may not have meant to shoot me, but he did."

When Sandra looked up, the expression on Theresa's face was one of lapse and indeterminacy. This was the first time they had met since Sandra's release from County, and neither of them seemed to recall what they wanted to tell each other.

After a few long, anxious moments, Theresa finally thought of something.

"I told Mom we wouldn't be here when she got back," Theresa said. "Maybe you should go along home and I'll call you later."

When Sandra put down her cup, she felt the bandages rustle underneath her blouse. The bandages were there to touch her skin when Tony couldn't. That's what the others could never understand, Sandra thought. Tony and I are always together, even when we're far apart.

"You tell Mom not to worry," Sandra said after a while. "I'm not so keen on seeing her again, either."

Sandra served out her parole with special marks for good behavior. She took a part-time job at the local nursery and, after Tony received a promotion from Guard Squad, they moved into their first apartment together, a two-bedroom furnished duplex in Burbank. Tony enjoyed painting and repairing things, and Sandra enjoyed plotting their weekly dietary regimens. The next two months turned out to be the most relaxing and rewarding period of Sandra's entire life.

Then, one bright winter morning, Sandra registered at Community College Extension, where most of the good courses were already filled. Eventually she settled for something called Theory of Poetic Composition and began taking home stiff, oversized paperback books by people with foreign, angular names such as Derrida, Lacan, Irigaray, and Homi Bhaba. There were no road maps or compasses in these books, and the sentences took you around in ever-diminishing circles, like rides in an amusement park nobody in their right mind would want to visit. Sandra sort of liked her reading assignments, though. The less she understood them, the more she figured she needed to learn. If there was one thing Sandra felt she needed in her life, it was a liberal education.

"Poetry is not an act," Sandra's instructor explained one night during a lecture on Metonymy as Metaphor. "Poetry is symbolic intention. It's not a thing, but a thing's representation. Poetry is the emergence of what *can be* from that which merely *is.* I love poetry and have loved it all my life. Especially when it deconstructs gender-specific stereotypes, or subverts class-based notions of hegemony and power."

Sandra sat entranced through the entire lecture, even while the rest of her fellow students were either asleep at their desks, or scribbling homework assignments for other classes. Perhaps this poetic theory stuff isn't such a big deal, Sandra thought. Perhaps it's something I've suspected all along.

"I really loved your lecture tonight, Timothy," Sandra told him later in the faculty staff room, where he invited her to share hot vended coffee and low-tar cigarettes. "It's really opened my eyes about things, especially my boyfriend, Tony, whom I live with. Tony is probably like the least poetical individual I've ever come across. Which is probably why I love him so much. Isn't *that* what you're trying to say?"

Timothy always nodded at whatever Sandra told him, as if he was already way ahead of her.

"Women are more intertextual than men," he told her simply. "That's because men have never progressed beyond the genital stage of ego development. Men're always trying to *get* something or *go* somewhere. While women are content with being wherever it is they already are."

The part that never made sense was that she hadn't even slept with Timothy; that was the weird part. And then Tony showing up in class that night, completely out of the blue. It didn't make sense. After all they'd been through together, how could Tony so thoroughly misunderstand?

For weeks after Tony's arrest, Sandra visited Timothy in his hospital room and brought him concise little offerings of fruit and candy. Timothy, though, hardly even acknowledged her presence. He certainly never thanked her for the gifts.

"I know it doesn't make sense, me bringing you things to eat and all. But I thought you could share them with the other patients. Or the nurses could mash up the chocolate and you could suck it off a spoon."

Timothy's hard, sullen silences were so selfish and inconsiderate, Sandra began to think he might not be quite so sophisticated as he liked to pretend. Rigged up to a set of pulleys and counterweights, he resembled one of those cyborgs in a science fiction movie. He certainly didn't show much more affection than one.

"Maybe I should bring you some baby food, Timothy.

Would you like that? Or some of those vanilla puddings that come in the little tin cans?"

There were times when Sandra wondered if there was anything she could do to make Timothy respect her again. There were other times, though, when she wished she had just stayed home.

"You're like the only friend I've got in the entire world," she told Tony during one of her visits to the California Men's Colony. She would take the 7:00 AM Greyhound from Burbank to San Luis Obispo, then catch the hourly shuttle outside County Courthouse. "It's like nobody returns my calls anymore. Not Mom, not Priscilla, not the girls from my old job. Last time I spoke to Theresa she told me, in this really snotty way, like, 'Nobody can help you, Sandra, until you learn to help yourself.' Now, what the hell did she mean by that? Since when have I ever asked, since when have I ever *needed*, anybody's help but my own?"

Back home, Sandra confronted the same intriguing absences. Tony's shaving things in the bathroom, his dirty T-shirts on the floor. Oil stains in the driveway, rusty golf clubs in the closet. Then one day Sandra dropped by the hospital to bring Timothy some magazines and encountered the biggest, most yawning absence of all.

"Mr. Tennyson?" the head nurse replied. "I'm afraid Mr. Tennyson checked out hours ago."

On her way back to the elevator, Sandra peeked into Timothy's room and saw the bed stripped down to a plaid Posturepedic mattress. All the plastic vases Sandra once filled with flowers were dry and empty now. Even the color TV had been removed from its bolts on the wall.

When the Department of Literature and Languages

wouldn't release Timothy's home number, Sandra began parking outside his office at the college, where she sat all day reading tabloid newspapers and drinking Vittel from a corrugated plastic container. After a few days of close observation she even learned to distinguish Timothy's fellow TA's from the permanent faculty. The trick was that TA's were often the same age as their students, but invariably drove lousier cars.

She knew he'd come back. Not like a criminal to the scene of his crime, but because he had this anal hangup about the books in his office. When she finally found Timothy again he was still wearing some sort of clamp-like device on the right side of his head, but he wasn't in his wheelchair anymore, and he hardly needed the crutches.

"I guess I've committed some pretty big boners in my life," Sandra told him. "I've gotten myself involved in some pretty dead-end relationships. But at least I always tried to be honest with my feelings, and I certainly never ran away from people, Timothy, which is obviously your way of dealing with things whenever they get too *complicated*. I mean, I'd rather make my own stupid mistakes in this life and take personal responsibility for them, instead of, you know, pretending the mistakes never happened, and hiding my head in the sand."

Timothy had retreated behind his massive steel desk. She couldn't tell if he was trying to increase the distance between him and her, or to decrease the distance between him and his books.

"It's really good to see you, Sandra. We should get together sometime. I'll call you, okay?"

"You don't need to lie to me, Timothy; I know you're too mean-spirited to forgive. I just wanted you to know that I've missed you since you went away. The funny part is, I don't even know what I miss about you. I just do."

Sandra cried all the way home in her car. She felt as if she had closed an important door in her life, and now she was standing in a dark hallway all alone. Then, when she turned onto her street, she saw the old familiar truck skewed across the driveway of her apartment building, blocking two other spaces and leaking oil on the asphalt. The engine was still ticking with heat, emitting a wavy mirage in the air.

It was so Tony it was unbelievable, Sandra thought. Some people just never *learned*.

"Where the fuck have you been?" he asked. He was wearing the same tank-top and jeans combination as the night they arrested him at the bowling alley. He had even found his old hunting knife, which Sandra had stowed with his high school sports memorabilia in the hall closet. "You've been with him, haven't you," Tony said again and again. "The whole time I've been locked up, you've been sleeping with *him*."

He kept waving the knife around and threw a dirty dish or two, but it wasn't the same anymore. Sandra sat on the sofa and lit a cigarette. While he stormed and fought for her attention, she issued one grayish exhalation after another, like a weird form of ellipses.

"Maybe this'll make you listen," Tony said, showing her the flat, dull knife. He placed it against her cheek so she could feel the coldness. Then he saw the even colder expression in her eyes.

Tony backed up a step. He looked at the knife in his hand. He seemed so sad that Sandra wanted to hold him—but not enough to actually do it.

"I just don't love you anymore," she told him. "I wish I did, but something's changed. I hope you'll understand."

They cried together for more than an hour. Then Sandra told Tony to leave.

"I've completely resolved myself against men for a while," Sandra told Theresa over the phone. "I'm not dating them, I'm not fucking them, I'm not letting them into my apartment, even to go to the bathroom. I'm making space for me and my own thoughts until I get things sorted. And I'm going to get things sorted without anybody's help but my own."

Theresa, though, wasn't much use in the support department. As per usual.

"I'm glad to hear it, Sandra," Theresa said. "But I'm sorry. I can't imagine you going two weeks without a man."

Sandra watched a lot of TV and tried to read good books. She concentrated on the dollar classics but usually couldn't get past the introductions, in which pompous professorial types waxed poetic about "stunning ambiguities" and "riddling enigmas."

"I'll give you a goddamn riddling enigma," Sandra would tell the book just before flinging it across the room. "Professor Timothy fucking Tennyson, that's what. He's a fucking riddling enigma and a half."

What made it worse was that everywhere Sandra went, the world was filled with couples, as if everybody had been matched off in some bizarre raffle to which Sandra hadn't even been invited to apply. Boy-girl, girl-boy, boy-boy, girl-girl. She saw them in the supermarket, she saw them in the bank, she saw them standing in line at the movies. Girl-boy, girl-girl, boy-boy, boy-girl. Sometimes Sandra would sit in her car in the parking lot of the

Golden West Mall and just count them going past. Couple, couple, couple, couple. Young teenage couples and really old, gnarly-looking couples. Couples with pony tails and couples pushing baby carriages. One-two, two-two, three-two, four-two. It was like what they used to tell her about in algebra—what was it, binary systems? In binary systems there were only two numbers worth counting. Then you started all over again.

It seemed like months since she'd sent Tony packing, but according to her checkbook calendar it turned out to be less than nine days. The fact that Tony had already moved in with a new girlfriend just made everything worse.

"You gotta have love," Tony told her one night on the phone. "Some kind or another, but love it's gotta be. None of us are experts, baby. We just do the best we can. Now, you didn't throw out my old hunting knife, did you? Or my old set of clubs? What I'll do is come by and collect them next week while you're at work. That way we won't have another one of our stupid old scenes."

That night Sandra loaded Tony's golf clubs into the passenger side of her car and drove to Community College. Night classes usually let out before ten, and by ten-fifteen Timothy was swinging his banker's box full of midterms into the trunk of his '73 Dodge. A young, slightly chunky blond girl in a summer dress was talking to him while she picked split ends out of her hair. Then Timothy opened the passenger door for her and they drove to the 405.

Timothy's right rear signal light was cracked, so Sandra had no trouble following. It also helped that Timothy drove like an old woman, probably because he was the sort of guy who had lived his entire life afraid of getting hurt.

"But getting hurt is part of it," Sandra whispered to

herself as she drove. "Because poetry isn't something you read about in books, Mr. Know-Everything Intellectual. Poetry is something you *are*."

When Sandra turned on the radio, the soft-rock station started playing three of her favorite songs, one right after the other, and she took it as a sign. By the time the last song finished she had already pulled up against the curb and killed her lights. She was watching Timothy, parked in his driveway, kissing away at his latest student conquest. Mr. Know-it-all Teaching Assistant, who'd never learned anything important in his entire life. Until, of course, the night Sandra decided to teach him.

"I'd rather be angry than lonely," Sandra said out loud to herself just before selecting Tony's scratchy nine-iron from the hard-used leather bag and climbing out of her car. "I'd rather announce my love out here in the middle of the street than hide in my house behind some stupid book. The problem with you, Timothy, is that you think everything's *symbolic*. But some things aren't symbolic at all, baby. Some things are *really* real."

Dazzle Redux

Despite all the burrs and bad weather, Dazzle lived a good life in the woods. He ate plenty of fresh fruit and vegetables, learned to take one day at a time, and raised the gangly pups of his common-law wife, Edwina, with as much genuine affection as if they were his very own. There were times, however, when Dazzle found that being a decent father figure took more patience than he could muster. And no matter how hard he tried to restrain himself, he couldn't stop telling everybody what to do.

"No, no, *no*," Dazzle told the twins for about the zillionth time that morning. "Let's try it again, okay? *This* is a rectangle. *This* is a rhomboid. And *this* is a circle." Dazzle sketched the shapes in the powdery red dirt as he spoke them, trying to show the twins that geometry was as graspable as any bone, stick, or rock. "Okay, Heckle, it's your turn. Let's pretend I've sent you on a top secret assignment. You're supposed to go down to the Land of Men and bring me a Frisbee. Have you got that, Heckle? Do you know what a Frisbee is?"

Heckle, who had been warming his cold nose under Jeckle's gravid belly, sat up with a start. He licked his wet lips hungrily.

"Just show me that Frisbee," Heckle snapped. "I'll whip that sucker out of the sky, no problem."

"Okay, boy," Dazzle continued. "Now take a deep breath and look at the shapes I've drawn. And tell me— which one's the shape of a Frisbee? Show me the circle. The circle is the *shape* of a Frisbee. Point to the circle and you win the game."

Dazzle spoke evenly, in short, compact sentences, as if he were marking a trail with bright red beads. But no matter how clearly Dazzle pointed the way, Heckle never managed to keep up for long.

"A circle is *like* a Frisbee?" Heckle wondered out loud, mewling and starting to twitch. "But *not* a Frisbee, really? A circle's a space on the ground when a Frisbee's not there? So what the hell do I want with a circle, anyway? Why can't I have a Frisbee instead?"

"You're thinking too hard, Heckle," Dazzle warned. "Relax, take a deep breath, and point to the circle. You can do it, boy. So do it for me now."

"This is *not* the Frisbee!" Heckle declared with a pounce. "Here it's *not*! This *isn't* it *here*!" Heckle was so slavery with confusion that he looked as if he had just chewed a frog. Within moments he had pawed the rhomboid completely out of existence—both metaphorically and literally.

Times like these Dazzle felt like wandering down to

PCH and hurling himself in front of the first eighteen-wheeler that came along.

"Not quite, Heckle," Dazzle pronounced finally, with all the parental patience he could muster. "But at least you pointed to a geometric figure, and not a dead beetle, like last time. So what say we sleep on it and take another shot in the morning. As I've told you many times before—Nietzsche's *Genealogy of Morals* wasn't written in a day."

"Maybe I'm not all I should be in the family skills department," Dazzle confessed that night to his erstwhile mate, Edwina. "But getting through to those kids of yours is like having a conversation with a block of wood, I swear. If I try to instruct them in the most basic math and science skills, they're not interested. If I try to teach them which way to look when crossing the street, they're still not interested. If I try to point out the most obvious cultural contradictions of multinational capitalism, why, just forget about it. They're *really* not interested. If you can't eat it or fuck it, it's not important; that's *their* attitude. And you want to know what pisses me off most? They may be *right*. Maybe fucking and eating really are the ne plus ultra of canine development. And in the long run of history, *I'm* the biggest fool in town."

Edwina was a pretty faithful bitch (at least since menopause), who had long provided Dazzle everything he considered crucial to a long-term relationship. She never questioned his judgment. She rarely bit him hard enough to draw blood. And she never once kicked him out of bed for snoring. At the same time, Edwina wasn't the sort of dog who knew how to hold up her end of a conversation. In fact, whenever Dazzle started pouring out his most heartfelt anxieties, she promptly curled into a fetal ball and fell fast asleep.

"Growwwl," Edwina muttered, her half-lidded eyes flickering out the weird morse of dreams. "Wolves aren't welcome 'round these parts. And neither are you mailmen."

Nevertheless, Dazzle found something infinitely comforting about a good night's sleep with Edwina. Her ambient heat soothed the knots in his shoulders, and her inattention dissolved the perplexities in his brain. As a result, Dazzle awoke every morning filled with fresh intentions and resolve.

"I'm going to be more understanding and thoughtful," Dazzle would assure himself, performing his ablutions in the piney-smelling creek. "And I won't be so quick to lose my temper, either." But once Dazzle had shaken himself dry with a few soul-rattling shivers and climbed back up the flinty hill, all such resolutions vanished with the breeze. He saw his lazy foster progeny licking themselves around the extinguished campfire. He smelled the unburied heaps of sour bones and dead mice. And he heard the casual yips of random lovemaking fill the rough-hewn settlement with a sort of ambient hum. ("Roll over, sweetheart," or "You kids go chase a gopher or something. Mom and Dad need a little alone time—dig?") If there was one thing that really got Dazzle's dander up, it was watching his fellow dogs take the best things in life for granted, such as liberty, well-stocked provisions, and properly functioning reproductive organs.

"Come on, guys!" Dazzle barked. "Wake up and smell the coffee, will you? You can't lie around in your own filth all day. Let me show you how to build a fire, or gather blueberries, or even compose a sestina. I mean, what good is all this free time if you don't know how to use it? And that means you, Heckle, so don't go skulking into those bushes. I want you to sit down with me right this minute and draw me a parabola. You're gonna learn your basic geometry, pal, or my name ain't Dazzle the Dog."

Over succeeding days and weeks, Dazzle tried counting to ten, positive thinking, and just plain walking away. But no matter how much he held back, he couldn't seem to go ten minutes without bossing his fellow dogs into a tizzy. Pretty soon the role of benevolent despot became as confining to Dazzle as any basement garage or backyard fence. And Dazzle, who couldn't bear the notion that he might be denying anybody (especially himself) true freedom, decided it was time to take another trip into the world.

"Basically," Dazzle told his assembled foster progeny on the day he left for LA, "I want you guys to stick together until I get back. Try not to eat so much red meat, keep an eye on your crazy mom, and don't let the pups go wild on you. Jeckle, stop hanging with coyotes. Stan, if you took a bath every few days or so, that rash of yours would clear up, no problem. And if for some reason I *don't* return from my ridiculous search for inner peace, I want you all to know that I love you, and I'm sorry I've been so temperamental these past few months. I guess there're still a few things I need to figure out in my life, and if I don't figure them out now, I probably never will. Oh, and one last thing. I've hidden the Cheetos under a blue log by the river, so do me a favor . . ."

But before Dazzle could complete his final instructions, the entire clan of foster pups and grand pups took off in one shaggy, collective flash. Without even a woof good-bye, they disappeared over the first low rise and were gone.

Dazzle tried not to feel hurt or disappointed. Dogs,

after all, were dogs. And by their very nature, dogs will do anything for a Cheetos.

"Try to save a few till I get back," Dazzle concluded softly through the swirling haze of dandruffy dog hairs. "Name-brand snack foods don't grow on trees."

"I guess I'm what you'd call your basic stay-at-home individual," Dazzle's dad confessed on the morning his estranged son appeared on his doorstep. "I like to sleep every night on the same blanket, make my daily rounds pissing on the same posts, and pretty much eat out of the same garbage cans every day of my existence. And with the exception of the occasional bitch in heat that staggers my way, I consider the high point of my life to be a really good bowel movement. Rock hard, intact, clean cut at both ends. I mean, what else *is* there? Sure, I sowed my share of wild oats. But now I just want to be left alone with my memories, my naps, and my happy scrounging in alleyways and garbage cans. Which, by the way, brings me to my next point, Mr. Doozle. Or did you say your name was Dizzle?"

"Dazzle," Dazzle replied weakly, trying not to look hurt.

"Whatever. Way I look at it, is maybe you could step back from my doorway just a tad. Not that I actually *doubt* your claim of kinship, mind you. But turn around slowly, that's it, and keep your paws where I can see them . . ."

Times like this, Dazzle didn't feel embarrassed for himself. He felt embarrassed for his entire species.

"Ah, yes," Dazzle's dad said, sniffing around in his son's private parts like a pig rooting out truffles. "That's *definitely* a smell I recognize."

"Things happened at the pound, Pop. You never gave me a chance to explain."

But of course it was already too late. Dazzle's dad emitted an abrupt snort of amazement and fell back, plop, onto his gray, flat haunches. His ice-cold nostrils flared.

"Jesus Christ, son. Somebody chopped off your balls!"

Dazzle sighed with a sad little shiver.

"Tell me about it," Dazzle said.

Pop invited Dazzle to spend the night in his sheltered alleyway outside a condemned Pizza Hut and even offered to share some of his moldier blankets and food stuffs. But he refused to acknowledge any moral responsibility for Dazzle's life. Or manifest the slightest degree of remorse.

"One thing I simply won't allow," Pop said, "and that's for you to make me feel bad about myself. Life's a mess, whichever way you look at it, and us dogs got to do anything we can to survive. Sometimes it means sucking up to human beings. Other times it means turning our backs on one another. In a better world, son, sure, I'd have stuck around, taught you a few things, provided for you and your sisters the best I knew how. But the world doesn't always allow us to do what we're *supposed* to. Sometimes we have to settle for what we *must* do instead."

"So why didn't you keep an eye on us, Pop?" Dazzle asked his father from time to time. "We were right down the street, living in a hole Mom dug behind the Lucky Market. All you had to do was walk down the street and say hello."

Dazzle's dad issued sighs like exclamations. He wasn't trying to make points, exactly. He was expressing the hard, breathy futility of saying anything at all.

"Your mom didn't want me around, sport. It would've only upset her."

"But what about after Mom went away? Why didn't you come visit then?"

"Because by that point you didn't want to see me anymore. And besides, I'd taken up with this wild bitch from Vanowen. You wouldn't have wanted me to abandon my responsibilities to *her*, now, would you?"

Sometimes, when Dazzle's inquiries grew a little bristly, Pop would shut off every avenue to discourse with a generic injunction. "No use rehashing the same refried beans," Pop would say. Or even, "Why don't we get some sleep and talk about it in the morning."

Dazzle's dad had grown so radically dissociated from his own feelings over the years that he didn't have any idea what terrible shape he was really in. He rarely bathed or picked up after himself. He ate nothing but day-old junk food foraged from back alley bins. And he never listened to a single word anybody tried to tell him, especially if it might do him good.

Every morning Dazzle's dad woke at dawn, lapped dirty water from a blocked drain, and set off for his diurnal scrounge. Meanwhile, Dazzle trailed along dutifully, like a cynical Boswell.

"Well, what have we here?" Dazzle's dad would proudly proclaim, as if he had just discovered the Northwest Passage. "Looks to me like a good-sized chunk of a double bacon cheeseburger, with a few crispy fries still attached to this melted cheese here, mmm. And if I remember correctly, son, you said we shouldn't even *look* in this can, right?"

Or, "Let's face it. Dogs are stupid, and humans aren't. That's why dogs live in ditches and eat garbage, and humans live in classy homes and can visit the McDonald's drive-through any damn time they please. I'm not trying to blow my own trumpet, kid, but you and I are rocket scientists compared to your normal dog. So complain all you want about my lousy child-rearing techniques. Without my brains, kid, you'd have ridden off with the first dogcatcher that showed you a biscuit. Just like your poor stupid mom."

Or, "Let's wander past this empty lot for a moment and see . . . ah, there he is. Inside that sewer drain resides Mad Dingo Dog, most completely unreasonable creature I've ever known. Best if you stay out of this neighborhood altogether, son. Lesson number one of urban living is don't worry about the humans. Keep a lookout for your fellow dogs."

Dear Edwina,

If you could read and I could write, I'd probably send you a letter much like the one you're holding in your paws right now.

Visiting Dad has turned out to be a total bummer. In fact, I've never met anybody so shut down and disaffected in my entire life. All Dad does these days is eat chocolate doughnuts, sleep, and evade the local dogcatcher.

I hope everything is okay with you and the kids. Despite my frequently cranky moods, I really miss my life with you in the woods. And I sure hope you'll all still be there when I get back.

Love,
Dazzle

Despite all his talk about freethinking individualism and so forth, years of bad faith had worn Pop's identity down to the nub. If he wasn't ranting about the SPCA or the poor quality of corporate-produced fast-franchise doughnuts, he just lay motionless on the concrete floor of his apartment for hours, staring morosely at the cobwebby pointillism of dead flies on the wall.

"What's bothering you, Pop?" Dazzle would ask, testing his dad for movement the same way curious children poke dead rabbits in the road with a stick. "What are you thinking about? Want to let me in on the big secret?"

"Nothing at all, son. Nothing I can't deal with, anyway."

"Don't you get lonely sometimes? Locked up in your own head?"

"Life is something you get through one day at a time, son. Stiff upper lip and all that."

"Why don't you try talking about it, Pop? When I'm feeling blue, I talk to Edwina, and it helps. Even when she doesn't understand a single word I'm trying to say."

"Talking about things doesn't make them better," Dazzle's dad replied simply, closing his eyes and scratching serenely behind one ear. "Now, if you don't mind, it's time for my afternoon nap."

Some days Dazzle felt as if he were sniffing around the perimeter of a vast, black moat filled with man-eating crocodiles. In the center of the moat stood a tall, brooding castle, elaborate with Gothic statues and hand carved paraphernalia. Dazzle knew his dad was standing in the middle of this castle, waiting for someone to let him out. But it was impossible to let Dad *out* until someone showed Dazzle the way *in*. Dazzle's dad didn't seem to understand this predicament one bit.

Then one afternoon Dazzle went for a lonely walk through the streets of his remote, blissless puppyhood. Fences, walls, garbage bins, stray auto parts, oil-stained asphalt, bricked-over windows, and board-hammered doorways. So far as Dazzle could figure, the civilized world was filled with tacky diversions that led you places you didn't want to go. It was like being lost in a maze where every juncture was rigged with electric wires—zap, zap. Every choice was a bad choice. And every bad choice made you feel it was all your fault.

"Too much dualism," Dazzle decided, "can drive anybody nuts. Even a fairly intelligent individual like Pop."

Eventually Dazzle found himself loitering outside the ramshackle hut of Dad's weird neighbor Mad Dingo Dog, and wondering if anybody was home. Dazzle was beginning to miss the company of other dogs, even if they weren't very bright or loquacious. At least Edwina and the kids speak the truth as clearly as their crude tongues allow, Dazzle reflected fondly. But these shut-down alpha males like Pop, Jesus. Give me a break.

Dazzle was so mired in his own reflections that he didn't notice when he was no longer alone. At first he just felt the hairs bristling on his neck. Then, with an involuntary growl, he looked up.

Mad Dingo Dog had a warty, prolonged face tufted with gray whiskers. He squinted at Dazzle for a moment, then took a perfunctory sniff at the intervening air.

"Why, I'll be a pussy's uncle," Mad Dingo Dog exclaimed. "You smell just like my long-lost nephew Dazzle the Dog!"

The weird thing was, Dazzle never even knew he had an uncle. And yet from the moment they met, they caught on like a house afire.

"Yeah," Mad Dingo Dog confessed, "your old man's a piece of work. But one thing's certain—he's always been real proud of you. 'My son got himself out of this rat race,' he's always bragging. 'My son was too good for this dump, so he split. My son this and my son that.' Jeez, the old fart never stops talking about you. So what are you doing back in the Valley, for Christ's sake? I heard you had your own condo in the woods, soapy hot tub and everything. And you were running the world's first all-canine high-tech retail outlet, or something crazy like that."

Hearing all this exaggerated gossip about himself made Dazzle feel meager by comparison. After all, Dazzle didn't want to talk about himself. Dazzle wanted to talk about *him*.

"Maybe I misunderstood what Dad was saying," Dazzle ventured after a while, "but the way he tells it, he and I are the only halfway intelligent dogs on the planet. And you're this crazy, rabid guy who howls at the moon and keeps trying to steal all his best doughnuts."

Mad Dingo Dog couldn't help smiling. It resembled an allergic twitch.

"Yeah, well," Mad Dingo Dog concluded wistfully. "That certainly sounds like your old man."

By the time Dazzle returned to Dad's condemned basement, he found a dogcatcher's van parked in the alley, and a pale, overweight dogcatcher leaning into Dad's doorway with a dog biscuit.

"Come here, old soldier," the dogcatcher was saying, "and I'll take you to the land of milk and honey. Free chow, plenty of furry friends to keep you company, and at the end of the day, a bonus injection of this really fine medication I've put aside especially for you. No more loneliness, bud. No more wondering what it's all about.

So come along, boy, that's a good dog, one more step, then another. Come get your biscuit. Then I'll drive you to the pound and teach you what real peace is all about."

In back of the idling white van a mangy assortment of alley strays were scrambling all over one another trying to get out. They yelped and howled and woofed and barked.

"Don't listen to him, guy!" an old gray bulldog cried, pawing the grated window. "It's hell in here!"

Dazzle stood and contemplated this weird scenario for a moment. His dad, the dogcatcher, strays in a van, and the hot Encino sun staring implacably down. He could barely hear Dad's whisper through the distant swish of traffic on 101.

"I don't want it to hurt," Dad whispered, his nose beginning to emerge from the doorway of his hovel. "I just want to go somewhere I don't have to think or feel guilty. And where nothing that happens is ever my fault."

"We'll give you oodles of peace and quiet, old boy," the dogcatcher replied softly. He spoke with the glib confidence of a man who really liked his job. "We'll take you to a place where you don't have to think about anything anymore."

"I thought I'd leave my apartment to my son. I don't think he wants me around anyway. I'm starting to get on his nerves."

"It's time for the old to make way for the new, pal. No point holding on to a world that doesn't want you. Come along with me and I'll take care of *every*thing."

For a brief moment, Dazzle thought that this was probably the sort of decision his dad should make for himself. But being a civil libertarian, he couldn't stand to watch the public service sector impinging on anybody's personal freedom. So without pondering the situation any farther, Dazzle trotted over to the municipal-issue van, climbed into the driver's seat, and activated the emergency door release with his paw. Behind him in the crowded cabin, the hairy clamor ceased.

Then, with a faint clang, the rear doors swung miraculously open.

"I don't know about you guys," the bulldog interposed, "but I'm outta here."

Wild dogs poured from the back of the van like marbles from the mouth of a jar, ricocheting off one another in every direction. The dogcatcher was so startled that he dropped his biscuit.

"Wait! Stop! Bad dog! Bad dog!" He was issuing shotgun proclamations and running down the alley. Eventually he turned the far corner and disappeared.

"Bad dogs to *you*, maybe," Dazzle said softly. "But to my way of thinking, they're just doing what dogs gotta do."

That night, after a lackluster celebratory bash of chocolate doughnuts and Diet Tab, Dazzle finally told his dissociative old dad the news.

"I'm sorry, Pop," he said, "but I can't stand to see you do this to yourself anymore. I had these illusions, right, that maybe we'd reach some sort of reconciliation, and maybe you'd even come home with me to the woods. But now I realize that you're so tied up in your endless routines and bad faith that you'll never let go. So what I'll do, see, is tell your grandkids you died. I'll tell them you sent your love, but that you rolled over and died shortly after I found you. I'll tell them you got hit by a car, or developed lung cancer from the smog, or got shot in the butt by some soiled kid with a BB gun. I'll use you as an example, Pop, of what urban America can do to a dog, and if we're lucky, maybe none of our semiprogeny will ever stumble into this hellhole you can't seem to leave. I won't kiss you good-bye or anything, but just say thanks for your hospitality and get my poor frazzled butt out of here. If I start now, I can maybe hit Ventura by morning."

Dazzle finished having his say with an expiring sigh. Ahh, Dazzle thought, I wasn't even angry or anything. I just had to tell him good-bye.

"So what is it, Pop?" Dazzle asked from the verge of the weedy doorway. Dazzle was wearing a painstakingly adjusted backpack slung over one shoulder; it contained a cheese sandwich, a stale jelly doughnut, and a half-liter bottle of Évian. "Am I taking off and you've got nothing left to say? Don't lose the moment, Pop. I've lost a few moments in my life and I can promise you one thing: you never get them back."

Dazzle's dad regarded his son with a slightly cocked expression, as if he heard distant birds singing somewhere.

Then, for the first time in his life, he finally told Dazzle what was really on his mind.

"Grandkids?" Dazzle's dad said. "You never said anything about grandkids."

So Dazzle took his dad home to the high mountains, where they never exchanged any true, heartfelt words ever again. After all, there's plenty of sunshine and fresh air to keep you occupied in the mountains. And sometimes talk just gets in the way of living.

"I guess I'll never be a perfect father," Dazzle confessed to Edwina one night, gazing out at the sky littered with stars. "Or a perfect son, for that matter. And when I die, there may not be another dog in the entire world who knows how to light the evening fire, or record the day's events for posterity. But history belongs to each generation to figure out for itself, so there's no point in me getting all worked up about things I can't change. Sometimes, old girl, a dog needs to stop wrestling with the world long enough to get on with the simple fact of living in it. Like you and me, Edwina. Living together— nose to haunch and haunch to nose."

It was a miraculous summer that Dazzle would remember fondly all his life. The pups grew progressively leaner, brighter, and more independent. Brisk sea winds kept the white sun cool. And wild wolves occasionally drifted into the orbit of their encampment, lured by aromas of toasted marshmallows and bitches in heat. It was a summer of perfect somnolence and irreflection. Except, of course, when it came to Dazzle's immutable dad.

"For crying out loud!" Dazzle's dad was often heard exclaiming through the warm, fir-scented air. "It's a rhomboid, for Christ's sake! Don't you idiots know what a *rhomboid* is?"

But it was one of the miracles of that particular summer that nobody ever figured out what a rhomboid was. Nobody even cared.

Penguins for Lunch

Though dabbling in all three elements, and indeed possessing some rudimentary claims to all, the penguin is at home in none. On land it stumps; afloat it sculls; in the air it flops. As if ashamed of her failure, Nature keeps this ungainly child hidden away at the ends of the earth.
—Melville, "The Encantadas"

The Ice Floe Bar and Grill

"I'm a high-flying entrepreneur on the free market of love," Whistling Pete told his closest friend, Buster Davenport, one sunny afternoon at the Ice Floe Bar and Grill. "You don't blame Bulgari for selling watches, do you? You don't blame McDonald's for frying burgers, or the Japs for peddling cheap cars. Well, what *I've* got just happens to be what the little girlies *want*. And when the little girlies want it, well, I don't mean to sound rude, Buster—but I happen to be *just* the guy that's going to give it to them."

The Ice Floe Bar and Grill belonged to a series of new upmarket franchise restaurants that had recently opened all across the tundra. As part of their inaugural promotion campaign, the Ice Floe was offering dollar margaritas during happy hour, along with all the free mackerel you could lay your flippers on.

Whistling Pete slid a creamy oyster down his throat and sighed. He patted his white belly, as if testing for tone.

"This is the life, Buster," he said philosophically, leaning back in his green vinyl lawn chair and folding his sleek, muscular flippers behind his head. He and Buster were sitting on a veranda overlooking the outdoor pool. "Sunny days, starry nights, envelopes of rich, fatty tissue to keep our butts warm, and loving spouses to go home to. What more could we ask? What more, that is, than maybe a hasty little frolic in the frost with one of yonder snow maidens?"

Nodding toward the various lithe penguinettes sporting themselves seductively around the pool, Whistling Pete click-clocked his tongue. His entire body shivered with a slow, delicious enthusiasm for itself.

"Yeah, well, I just hope you know what you're doing," Buster said, his gaze roving back and forth across the patio. Then he glanced sheepishly over his shoulders, as if he expected their indignant wives to appear at any moment.

When the waitress came up to ask, "How you boys doing?," Buster nearly jumped out of his socks.

"Whoa there, Buster. Relax, old buddy. It's not the *gendarmes.*" Whistling Pete cautioned his friend with an upraised flipper and presented the waitress his award-winning smile. "And how are *you* doing this afternoon, sweetie?"

"If you boys don't need anything," she said, "I'll go check my other tables."

Buster, slightly out of breath, was still smoothing his ruffled tail feathers. "I guess I'll have another margarita," he said, looking forlornly at his empty white side dish. "And if happy hour's still on, could you maybe find us some more mackerel?"

Whistling Pete unashamedly examined the waitress's fatty deposits.

"Me," Whistling Pete added, "I'll have some of what *she's* having."

He indicated a large commercial advertisement posted behind the bar. It featured a curvaceous, dimpled penguinette scantily clad in a white silk top hat and baggy white fishnet stockings. She was leaning against a sporty red snowmobile and stroking a large, icy bottle of Smirnoff's.

The bold black caption exclaimed: IT'S PENGUINIFIC!

While Buster resumed his edgy lookout for wives, Whistling Pete watched their waitress waddle back to the bar.

"Vah-vah-vah-*voom*!" he said and saluted her departing buttocks with the dissolving slush in his glass. Then he tossed it down with his last oyster slider. His toes evinced a self-satisfied little wriggle.

"Life's definitely the coolest," Whistling Pete pronounced. "The sun rises, the sun sets. And so do I, Buster, old pal. So do I."

Whistling Pete slammed down his glass with a familiar emphasis.

"Yeah, well." Buster's eyes flicked from entrance to exit, from restroom to window to door. He picked up the extinguished mackerel plate and sadly licked it.

"I just hope you know what you're doing," he said.

Whistling Pete arranged for a clandestine rendezvous with one of his ladies nearly every day at noon, just when the twilit sky was beginning to generate something like phosphorescence. They met unashamedly at the Ice Floe for drinks and quick, light lunches while Pete proferred flowers, compliments, stockings, and chocolates. Then, as fast as their little legs could carry them, they dashed next door to the Crystal Palace Motel, where Whistling Pete kept an open account. They ordered caviar and champagne through room service, sported themselves silly across the taut-fitted coverlets, and made the most they could of an hour—sometimes an hour and a half.

"This is the life," Whistling Pete muttered every so often. "This is what the Almighty Penguin had in mind when he designed such cute little penguinettes."

Infidelity took all the knots out of a morning. The bad breakfast with the screaming baby, the frantic rush of late orders at the warehouse, and the sense of blue, dissolute formlessness Pete experienced whenever he gazed out his office window at the black morning sky littered with cold, white stars.

"It's the worst weather in the entire universe," Pete regularly complained to his morning mug of Earl Grey. "Icicles, icebergs, ice mountains, and ice rocks. I'm not ashamed to say it. Antarctica sucks, even for penguins."

Then, looking up, he might find himself exchanging a quick, illicit glance with Berenice, the Accounts secretary across the hall.

After a moment, Berenice would smile and wave. After another moment, Whistling Pete would smile and wave back.

One of these days, Pete reminded himself, I really must chat up our little Berenice.

The penguinettes he did chat up were invariably young, impressionable, intelligent, and quick to please. Some of them worked in Whistling Pete's office at Consolidated

Fish, but mostly he met them during happy hour at cocktail lounges, or while swimming in local ponds. They were office girls in a hurry to be young and didn't bother themselves too much about moral imperatives or social graces.

"I just figure we have nice times together," Whistling Pete's favorite female, Melody Long, frequently explained, usually after her second gin and tonic and a quick romp in the motel sauna. "So maybe you're married and have kids—that's cool. I'm not a material girl. I don't need, like, to *own* a boy just because I *like* him."

Then, with a bubbly flirt and a giggle, she pinched Pete's belly with one flipper and soothed his inflated pride with the other.

"Not that we can call our little whistler a *boy*, exactly," she reminded him, nibbling at one of his stray chest feathers. "Mr. Pete is more what you'd call a dirty old *bull*. Isn't that right, cutey? Isn't that right, you big, bad boy, you?"

Lunchtime was what Whistling Pete lived for—brightness, intoxication, energy, and truth. Lunchtime was passion and glory. Lunchtime was life.

By the time Pete returned to his office he was already subsiding into a postcoital melancholy that wasn't altogether unpleasant.

"Hey there, bro," Buster said, leaning into Pete's office at about 4:00 PM The day's tentative flare of sunlight was already extinguishing. Weird refractions cast themselves across the planes of ice like spinning crystal discs. "We hitting happy hour today or what?"

Buster was already glancing anxiously over both shoulders. He was not the sort of penguin who pursued life head on.

Whistling Pete removed his feet from the desk and sat

up in his spring-cocked office chair. He saw the binders and ledgers, the interoffice memos, and the gray, slimy faxes. This desk, this office. These hours measured by dollars, these spaces demarcated by ice.

"Buster, old pal," Pete said finally and clapped his flippers together with brisk authority, "has the sun stopped shining or the earth ceased to spin? Of *course* we're hitting happy hour. And if I recall correctly, it's your turn to pick up the tab."

Making Marriage Work

"It's just a phase Pete's going through," Estelle said and regurgitated chunky blue broth into a white ceramic bowl. "Ever since he turned middle-aged, he can't seem to sit still. He stares at himself in the bathroom mirror all morning, combing his feathers and picking his beak. And every day on his way home from work he forgets to pick things up at the store—milk, bread, mineral water, you name it. He's wandering around in a dream world, Sandy, I swear. I know I should be angry, but I can't help feeling sorry for him. He's going through some pretty heavy emotional changes right now."

Estelle dabbed her beak with a pastel napkin. Then she passed the bowl to their six-month-old fledgling, who was conducting a happy inner sympathy with an upraised wooden ladle.

"Fish," Junior exclaimed. "Fish-*fishy*-fish."

Estelle sighed. Then, almost imperceptibly, belched.

"Excuse me," Estelle said.

Buster's wife, Sandy, lit another menthol cigarette and shook out her paper match with bristly impatience.

"For chrissakes, Estelle. Read the writing on the *wall*, will you? Your lousy husband's out fertilizing every yolk in town. What are you—*blind?*"

Estelle gazed out the sparkling window and sighed, leaning her beak on one cocked flipper. Sometimes she just wanted to sit in her clean kitchen, watch the thin sunlight, and feel the deep, immanent warmth of her own body. She was so bulked up with raw meat after months of gravid gorging that she could hardly waddle to the sink without losing her breath. And now Sandy, forever lean and mean, was telling her what to do with her life, as if she were some sort of expert.

"You don't understand," Estelle said. "If you want to make marriage work, then some things aren't that simple."

"Things *are* that simple, Estelle. And let me tell you how simple they are. Pete's screwing every cow on the island. He's dipping his wick in every candle on the beach. You can either tell him to shape up or move out. Or you can hack him to death with the stainless steel. I'll tell you one thing," Sandy said, punctuating her resolve by flicking a long, intact gray ash onto the checkered tablecloth, "if Buster ever pulled a fast one on me, boy, I'd bite out a firm message in his fat butt. That's what I'd do."

Estelle wanted to explain, but she couldn't work up any words from her overloaded body. It was strange how flesh could reshape itself around you, as if it possessed a mind of its own. Estelle looked at the flaring brightness outside. Then she looked at her six-month-old fledgling, Pete Junior, and reprovingly thumped the side of his high chair.

"Don't *play* with your food, mister," she said.

Caught in midgargle with a bolus of macerated mussel, Junior swallowed abruptly. He looked at his mom with wide eyes and put down his wooden ladle.

"Fish," he said evenly, indicating his chunky broth. "*Mum's* fish."

"Yes, baby," Estelle said slowly. "Mum's fish."

Lowering her head, Estelle began to cry. Softly at first, but with rising intensity, like the sound of distant winter thunderclaps.

Sandy bit off another tiny puff from her menthol cigarette. She looked at Junior, and Junior looked at her.

"There, there, honey," Sandy said. "It'll be all right. There, there."

And extinguishing her cigarette in the glass ashtray, Sandy took Estelle gently in her arms.

Some days, Whistling Pete didn't have any patience for family life. Grocery bills, diaper services, overpriced podiatrists, peeling linoleum, and faulty pipes. "Domesticity is for the birds," Pete pronounced solidly, walking home with Buster through the starry night. Atmospheric strobes wheeled across the black sky like chapters out of Revelation. "I'm talking about the feathery, flighty kind of birds, you know? The ones with their heads in the clouds? Sure, it *sounds* nice and all—big tract houses, gas central heating, indoor plumbing, and all that. Trade, commerce, certified schools for the kids, community rep, all the bread in one basket, *that* sort of domesticity, *you* know. But basically, man, it's an idea cooked up by the girlies. Wives, man; females seeking security for their babes. Girlies are home *builders*, but us guys, we're like home *breakers*. It's not our *fault*, Buster; it's just our nature. Girlies like home and hearth, three square meals, new wallpaper for the nursery, church weddings, and matching cutlery. Us guys, however, we're hunters and gatherers. We don't want cornflakes for breakfast; we want the hot blood of the kill in our mouths. We want to venture *beyond* what we know, and stop remembering all the boring places we've already been. Nature's *cruel*, Buster, just like *us*. Nature's cruel, and *so* are us guys."

The long, white road descended to the village, leading Pete toward the smell of yeasty bread baking. He saw yellow light glowing in the windowpanes of his house, and the idea that he was anticipated made him feel edgy and ungallant. Three strange minds waiting in a house where he didn't belong. They knew he was coming. He was already late.

He put his arm around Buster with a comradely squeeze and gestured downhill. "There it is, buddy. Our little village in the snow, the home our forefathers and foremothers planted in the wilderness. Back in the old days, our ancestors waddled around on *rocks*, man. They starved, hunted, mated, and died without proper funerals, and the only education they ever got came from the School of Hard Knocks. And who do you think initiated the idea of *houses*, man? Why, the *ladies*, of course. 'Let's stack a few ice blocks over there as a sort of lean-to,' they told their weary, flatulent old husbands. 'How about four walls, honey? A roof and a floor?' Us guys would have lain out there scratching our lice on that stupid rock forever if *we'd* had the choice. But the choice *wasn't* ours, buddy. No way."

Buster, well oiled with budget tequila, was waddling along beside Pete with uncustomary resolution. Instead of glancing over his twitchy shoulders, he gazed dreamily into the endlessly illuminated sky. Showers of meteors, swirls of galaxies, planets entrained by moons and whorling dust. Buster loved the night when it got like this: vast, unencompassable, and rinsed with sensation.

"Actually," Buster muttered out loud, "I always kind of dug domesticity. Beds with sheets, down comforters, canned lager, and imported salsa. I like knowing I'll get paid every Friday, as regular as clockwork. Some days, Sundays especially, I lie in my warm bed and just let my mind wander. I don't go anywhere. I just let my imagination loose and I *wander*."

Pete whistled softly to himself. He was thinking: Melody, Marianne, Gwendolyn, and Jane. Tomorrow at noon and next Wednesday at twelve forty-five. While Pete's body waddled down the steep slope toward the hard, unendurable village, his mind journeyed into different realms altogether. Places filled with thrill and expectation. Places of slow tongue and undress. At times like these, Pete believed he would never die. Even when the hard village stopped enduring, Whistling Pete wouldn't.

"Men build the cities," Pete said softly just before they arrived at his white doorway, his paved driveway, his leaning mailbox. "But believe you me. It's the girlies who make us live in them."

Despite his claims to the contrary, Pete arrived home each night aching with apology and self-reproach.

"I *know* I should have called," he told her. "I *know* it's late, and I forgot to buy milk again. And yes, I *did* drink too much, and spent too much, and Little Petey's gone to bed again without kissing Daddy good night. I'm sorry, Estelle, I really am. I'm sorry, but I can't seem to explain. Some nights I just have to get out with my buddies, have a few drinks, and unwind. No, and I can't promise it won't happen again. I wish I could, Estelle, but I can't."

Later, in bed, Estelle pretended to sleep. Pete could feel

the slow breath of the hard house around them, the ticking radiators and ruminating clocks. Next door in the nursery, Little Petey, true to his genotype, whistled faintly in his sleep.

"I'll try to be better," Whistling Pete told his wife, pretending he believed her when she pretended not to hear. "But that doesn't mean I'll succeed. Sure, I could always *tell* you what you want to hear, Estelle. But that doesn't mean I can *be* somebody I'm not."

Then, too tired for remorse, he fell asleep. And descended into his dreams of the Crystal Palace Motel.

"Of *course* I worry about Estelle and Junior," Buster told his wife that night, tossing and turning among the knotted sheets and lumpy pillows. "But Pete's my *friend*, Sandy. I'm not going to lie here and listen while you trash him."

"*Trash* him?" Sandy said in a rising crescendo of disbelief. "*I'm* trashing *him?*"

Buster turned onto his other side and gazed out the bare, glistening window. The full moon glowed like a primitive mandala.

"What about *Estelle*, huh? Who's trashing *her*, Buster? Who's doing the *serious* emotional trashing around here? *Me*, or your close *friend*, Whistling Pete?"

Buster submitted with something like relief. Sandy was like a geyser or an earth tremor. He had been hearing her about to happen all day.

"So I guess poor little Estelle is just supposed to grin and bear it—is *that* what you mean? Because if she calls her wonderful husband a liar, then she's *trashing* him? And if *I* start calling him a *louse*—which is exactly what he *is*, Buster—then *I'm* trashing him, too? I guess if it's a *man* doing the trashing, then that makes it okay, huh? Is *that* what you're saying, Buster? If *men* trash *women*, then that's the proper order of things, *right?*"

Buster took a long, deep breath and sighed.

"That's not what I said, Sandy. That's not what I said and you know it."

Every morning after a fight, breakfast became a ceremony of courtesy and burned toast. While Sandy brought in bottles of frozen milk from the front porch and thawed them on the stove, Buster read through yesterday's ice-hockey scores, enjoying the cool comfort of abstractions, a sort of rousing, statistical hum. Click, clicka-click-click. Clicka-click-click.

"I'm going shopping," Sandy announced flatly, peering at him across her china teacup.

"That's a good idea," Buster said, nervously glancing at the wall clock. In another few minutes he could leave for work without appearing obvious.

"I'm getting a beak trim and a pedicure at Valerie's. Then I'm meeting Estelle for lunch at the Green Kitchen."

Buster was afraid to look up from his paper.

"Have a nice time, honey," he said. "Give my best to Estelle."

Later, traipsing up the long, winding road to the factory, Buster rehearsed his concern until it resembled indignation, gesturing severely with his red metal lunch pail.

"Enough's *enough*," he said out loud to himself. "And I'm telling you this for your own good, Pete. If it was just a little fling every now and then, *that* might be understandable. But these daily rallies of yours are just *too much*. Show a little discretion, man. What do you think we are, *seals* or something? Happy flappers lying on the beach all day, mating indiscriminately, barking like morons? No, Pete, we've built something for ourselves out here. Homes and schools and factories and jobs. So if you want to shoot off your mouth about how rotten civilization is and all, well, that's your prerogative. But if you're going to continue *living* in it, then you've *got* to start taking responsibility. I hate to be so hard on you, bro'— believe me, I don't like it any more than you do. But I'm being hard on you because I *care*. And if you don't understand that, well, forget it. Maybe I've been wasting my time with you all along."

Steaming with resolution, Buster chugged into the factory just as the second whistle blew. Grizzly fishermen were dragging weirs full of squirming carp and tuna from the harbor while the factory gates were rolled open by large, muscly penguins in greasy gray overalls.

By the time Buster reached Pete's office, he knew he was going to do it. He was going to give Whistling Pete a piece of his mind. The hot words carried him up the stairs and down the hall, through Payroll, Group Insurance, and Human Resources, past filing cabinets, bulletin boards, and water fountains. Buster was going to speak his mind. Come hell or high water.

Inside Pete's office, Nadine, the Accounts secretary, was stirring a big pot of tea with a wooden spoon.

"Let me speak to Whistling Pete," Buster told her. "And tell him I'm talking *muy pronto*."

Nadine looked at Buster, then at the open door to Pete's office. She smiled faintly, as if she had been expecting this little display all morning.

"Sorry, Buster," Nadine said, "but Petey's not around." Then she placed the teapot on a wooden tray alongside four chipped ceramic mugs, one tarnished teaspoon, and a

bowl of brown, lumpish sugar. "But if it's an emergency—
and it better be one hell of an emergency—you can always
leave him a message at the Crystal Palace Motel."

Mordida Girls

Spring returned, and the squat white sun wouldn't leave,
skating around the horizon's meniscus of thinning ice and
dripping mountains like a sentry. Time grew increasingly
diffuse, gray, immeasurable, and abstract.

Not that time mattered to Whistling Pete anymore—
only the quick lapse into timelessness he regained every
afternoon in the arms of his adorable penguinettes. Often
he trysted two or three in a single afternoon, bang bang
bang, beginning each session with a few shots of Jack
Daniels and a plate of imported caviar. By the third or
fourth session he would fall rudely asleep and dream of
white, sandy beaches and tropical heat. Later he woke
alone in a dim room, saw the windows hung with thick
black curtains like a shroud, and heard the hissing radiators. Hotel personnel knocked summarily at the door.

"Maid service," said a woman in a heavy Dutch accent.
"Should we clean up, mister? Or you want we should
come back later?"

By the time Pete waddled into work it was as late as
three or three-thirty. Fellow administrators and their
assistants looked up distantly when Pete skirted through
the halls. Back in Accounts, Nadine was always in a terrible temper.

"Mr. Oswald came by from Marketing, and Joe Woz-
niak asked again about your expense receipts. I've *tried*
covering for you as far as the sales conference, but I can't

do anything if I don't see some retail brochures pretty soon. Oh, and your wife and little boy popped round asking for you—you were supposed to take your son fishing today. I think you blew it, Pete. Your wife seemed pretty upset."

"Oh, shit," Whistling Pete muttered, slumping into his swivel chair. He checked his vest pocket for a stray cigarette but located only twisted bits of tobacco and a small white business card. The card said:

Henrietta Philpott
Public Relations Consultant

He wondered if they had spent any time together. Or if maybe they were about to.

"I *knew* I'd forgotten something," Whistling Pete said.

Pete continued making excuses, but they felt more like formalities.

"I'm *going* to take Junior fishing," he declared. "I *want* to teach him how to fish. But I got delayed with a distributor on the Ronne Ice Shelf. What do you want me to do—neglect my job?"

"I sure wouldn't want that," Estelle said emptily, leaning against the kitchen table. She held a mackerel cracker in front of her face like a cue card. "Obviously your job's all you care about anymore. So tell that to your year-old son who adores you."

"I'll make it up, sport—I really will." Pete paced back and forth in the living room while Junior lay on the floor, perusing his geography homework (*Fishing Routes of Our Polar World, twelfth edition*). "We'll go camping, that's it. A weekend on the South Orkneys. Just you, me, and those mackerel. We'll bring along that new sealskin pup tent we've been meaning to try."

Junior didn't look up. He tapped a pencil against his beak and turned the page of his textbook. In the past few months since being weaned, his body had grown angular and weirdly composed. It wasn't a body that Pete recognized anymore.

"Like, it's *cool*, Dad. It's no big deal. We'll go fishing some other time. When you're not so busy, that is."

"I've *got* the expense receipts," Pete told the executive directors in the factory Green Room. "Of *course* I've got the expense receipts." They had called him in during lunch break, sitting around the long, black conference table munching processed-salmon sandwiches and prawn-flavored potato chips.

"It's just that, well, Payroll screwed up the group finance report, and by the time I got it straightened out it was time for the monthly service catalog and, well, I *know* it sounds like a bunch of half-assed excuses and all"—a bright sweat broke out on Pete's forehead, and he felt a faint dizzying rush, as if he were falling through vortices of warm air—"and of course I'll get the reports to you by Friday, and I'm not trying to divert blame or anything, right, 'cause Nadine's a great girl but she *does* have something of a temperament, blaming everything on the *system* and the male-dominated patriarchy and all that and, well, it's sort of hard to get her to cooperate so far as her official duties are concerned. I'm not blaming Nadine for the screwups, understand. I'm just saying I've only got two flippers, right?"

But no matter how hard Whistling Pete expostulated, prevaricated, and fibbed, he knew the game was coming to a close. Even though he had received a new company checkbook just two weeks ago, it was already used up from paying last month's motel, room service, and bar bills, and just as this month's bills were falling due, Finance was telling him they couldn't provide another checkbook until mid-May. He was going through each day in a weird somnambulism, never certain of the time, suffering from sinus headaches and blurred vision.

A line from an old Dylan song kept recurring to him: "To live outside the law you must be honest." What Pete interpreted it to mean was: "To live outside the law, you must work really, really hard." He woke every day at seven, gulped black coffee, and hurried to the factory, where he unsuccessfully tried to catch up with the work he had been neglecting for weeks. Then he would fall asleep at his desk, awaken to Nadine's puttering, and skip off in a faint anxiety rush to the Crystal Palace Motel, where he encountered the silk-clad bodies of Stella, Ariadne, Velma, and Chlöe. He returned home each evening through a slow, dull haze of incertitude to be greeted by unpaid bills, humming kitchen appliances, and intricate silences. Estelle in bed with her book. Junior out gallivanting with his friends.

Some nights Pete found the bedroom door bolted shut and knocked politely like a timid solicitor.

"Estelle?"

"What?"

"Are you in there?"

"Of course I'm in here."

"Can I come in?"

"No, you can't."

"I'm really bushed, Estelle. I need to lie down."

"Sleep on the couch."

"I feel really strange, you know, all run down and everything. I've got stomach pains, my liver's enlarged, there may be something wrong with my spleen. I'm really beat, Estelle, and I think, well—maybe we should talk."

"There's nothing to talk about," Estelle said with calm conviction, as if she were slipping a form letter under the door. "I'm afraid the time for talking is over."

Her voice was clipped and regular, like the factory's canning machine. Whistling Pete leaned against the flimsy plywood door.

"Oh, Estelle," Pete said with a sigh, feeling his entire body slump into itself like an expiring party balloon. "Maybe you're right, honey. Maybe there's nothing left to talk about at all."

"If you don't mind my saying, Pete, you're starting to look pretty thin and unraveled."

Melody was sitting on the edge of the mattress and pulling on her baggy fishnet stockings.

"I do what I can," Whistling Pete said dreamily. He imagined himself floating downriver on a jagged platform of ice. He was gazing at the white sky, the thin white sun and moon. "Sometimes I just can't seem to keep up."

Melody gazed distantly at herself in the shimmering vanity mirror. "You're starting to lose a little of your whaddayoucallit? Your joie de vivre. I don't mean to sound impolite or anything, baby, because we've had some great times together. But I just don't look forward to seeing you anymore. I mean, when I know we've got a date coming up—how do I say this? Knowing I'm going to see you is getting to be a serious bummer."

Melody anchored the tops of her stockings to a matching pair of elasticized red velvet garters.

"Even General Motors suffers an occasional financial slump," Whistling Pete said, smiling fondly at the clock on the wall. "Even the Japanese experience recessions."

Melody pulled on her short black cocktail skirt with a wriggle and scowled faintly at herself in the vanity mirror.

"I worry about you, Pete, I really do. You used to be *fun*. You used to be a lot of laughs. What happened to the *old* Whistling Pete? The guy who knew how to show a lady a good time?"

Pete gazed out the window at tall white mountains, gaping crevasses, rust-red lichen the size of dinner plates. We've lived for thousands of years, the lichen collectively muttered. And want to know what's happened in all that time?

Nothing nothing nothing nothing.

"I'll be fine," Pete said. He reached for his glass of Smirnoff's. "A bit of a bug, that's all. I'm working too hard. Need to start taking my vitamins."

"Yeah, well." Melody got up and brushed herself off. She was wearing a lot of crushed black velvet and pink powdery body blush. "You take care of yourself, Petey, because I worry about you, I really do. But until you get your act together, I think maybe we shouldn't see each other for a while. I hate to sound hard and insensitive, but I'm the kind of girl who needs to make the most of what she's got while she's still got it. And lately, Petey, you're just not the kind of guy who can help."

The Crystal Palace Motel

Buster sat at the Ice Floe sipping a strawberry margarita while Al the portly bartender swabbed everything down with a damp dishcloth.

"He's been over there every night," Al said. He shifted a toothpick from one side of his beak to the other and nodded in the direction of the Crystal Palace Motel. "And when he comes in here—usually for another bottle of Smirnoff's—he doesn't say hi or nothing. He just takes what he needs and leaves."

"No skin off my butt," Buster said and lit another menthol. Buster had recently taken up smoking, just to give his hands something to do. "He doesn't need my help. He's got his little girlies to keep him company."

"Little girlies," Al said and poured himself a soda water from the hand dispenser. "And God knows what else."

After lunch and a second strawberry margarita, Buster tried calling Pete's room at the Crystal Palace Motel, but there wasn't any answer. When he stopped by the lobby on his way back to work he found the day clerk playing a new handheld electronic ice-hockey game. The day clerk swung the beeping computer toy back and forth, as if he were steering a particularly nasty slalom down the rocky hillside of his imagination.

"Is Whistling Pete still in room 408?" Buster asked. Buster lit a fresh cigarette off his old one, and crushed the old one out in a hip-high, sand-filled aluminum ashtray.

"Ah *shit*," the day clerk said.

The computer beeped its tiny contempt and the day clerk looked up.

"Whistling Pete, huh?" He gave Buster the once-over. "He's not the sort of guy who has many friends. You must be another customer, right?"

Before he knew what he was doing, Buster was lifting the stroppy, bell-hatted little penguin up over the countertop and slamming him rudely against the clattery ashtray.

"What's *that* supposed to mean, numb nuts?"

"Hey, I was kidding is all."

Buster heard a tone in his own voice he didn't recognize.

"I'll ask you one more time," he said simply, "and don't give me any more blather. Just tell me where I can find my friend Whistling Pete."

The day clerk had come clean, leaving Buster to feel irredeemably dirty.

"You know what I'm talking about, mister—don't play innocent with me," the day clerk said, hitching up his uniform blue-serge slacks with a little swagger. "I'm talking seals, man. Otters. Big, slimy lady walruses with fat, blundery asses. It's like the tart's grand national around here—them strutting their stuff up and down those stairs day after day. And your pal, Mr. Pete, he doesn't leave the room at all anymore. You can't *imagine* the sort of disgusting activities going on in there. Sick is what it is. There should be a police ordinance or something. Not to mention the hotel tab, which has gotten completely out of hand."

Buster took the service elevator and arrived at a long, angular hallway dingy with infrequent lighting, where linty velour carpets emitted an unsavory sheen. The entire area smelled of cigarettes and spoiled vegetables.

When Buster knocked at room 408, he heard a slow, slumberous rouse from inside.

He coughed awkwardly. Then he knocked again.

"Yeah, well, it's not paradise," Pete conceded. "But then, who's looking for paradise, right, Buster?" He was sitting on the edge of his frayed, sunken mattress, scratching his genitals through tatty checkered boxer shorts. The room was littered with bottles, newspapers, and fast-food wrappers.

"Why don't you take a shower, Pete. Put on some clean underwear, for godsake. Then I'll take you home to your wife and your kid."

"My wife and my kid are history, Buster. Estelle took Junior to her sister's on the Fimbul Ice Shelf."

Buster refused to be deterred. If Pete was to have faith in himself ever, Buster would have to teach him how.

"First we'll get you squared away," Buster said. "Then we'll bring her back. She still loves you, Pete. I know she does."

"Bring her back to what?" Pete asked. His voice was phlegmy. He picked a white, sticky substance from his left ear and wiped it on the mottled sheets. "What's left of me ain't exactly a work of art, you know. And you must have heard about the expense money I embezzled. Nadine getting fired for my incompetence and graft. The fact that I've lost what little reputation and self-respect I had left— and the funny thing is, I don't give a goddamn. I don't miss any of it. Especially not the self-respect."

Buster, embarrassed by the false assurances that kept crossing his mind, looked away. He saw the messy bathroom, the broken, dripping toilet, towels on the floor.

"We'll find you a new job," Buster said. The lie echoed hollowly in the filthy room. "With Estelle and Junior's help we'll get you back on your feet again. Hell, buddy— *I* can loan you a few bob till you get yourself straightened out. What are friends for, huh?"

"Oh, Buster," Pete said with a sigh. "Wake up and smell the coffee, will you?" Pete indicated his entire body with a small ironic flourish. The high strain of ribs, the frazzled patchy feathers, the haunted and thinning gleam in his eyes. "All my nice sleek body fat melted away. No job, no family, no savings to speak of. It's ironic, really.

Because civilization has given me the luxury of thinking, I've had time to disrespect all the civilized comforts that allow me to think."

"Don't," Buster said. He knew he was in trouble if Pete started talking. "Stop it, Pete. Stop winding yourself up."

Pete was on his feet again, waddling back and forth in front of the bed. "But that's the *point*, isn't it? What do you build when you build yourself a civilization? Nice warm houses, nice warm restaurants, nice warm places to go to the bathroom. What does civilization give us, Buster? Temperature. Heat. Oxygen. Light. And what do we do with all this, this *energy*, this year-round fat and reserve? We burn it, pal. We use it to stoke the fire of our bodies all day and all night. We are burners of hard fuel, Buster, and thinkers of hard thoughts, and we can't ever rest until we die. Civilization doesn't solve problems, Buster. It reminds us of all the problems we haven't yet solved. What we don't have. Who we haven't been. How much we haven't spent. How many girlies we haven't plugged. It doesn't end, Buster. I keep thinking it *will* end, but it *doesn't* end. Not really."

"Don't do this to yourself," Buster said. "Give yourself a swift kick in the backside and shut your damn brain *off*."

Pete came to a sudden halt and he turned. His face was sunken, his eyes lit with a fire that burned itself as much as the things it touched.

"But Buster," he said, "the only way to turn it off is to stop living. The only way to forget what you know is to pretend not to be."

At which point Whistling Pete fell to the floor with a terrible crash.

With friends from the Ice Floe, Buster transported Pete back to his home, where the atmosphere had grown as stale, sluggish, and unreal as Pete's room at the Crystal Palace Motel. The walls, beds, and furniture were icy with neglect and disuse. The pilot light had extinguished in the furnace, and a shutter in the bedroom had ruptured under the impact of a recent storm, permitting an avalanche of rocky sludge to build up around the dressing table. The only whiff of life remaining was exuded by the bowels of the refrigerator, where shriveled vegetables and garlic bulbs blossomed. When they laid him out on the cold bed, Pete tossed and turned in his delirium, muttering against the tide of visions only he could save himself from. Buster couldn't reactivate the pilot light in the furnace, but he did manage to get a good blaze going in the hearth.

"More," Whistling Pete murmured. "More yesterdays. More tomorrows. Please please."

"Sleep tight, old buddy," Buster said, posting himself in a cracked wooden chair beside the bed. He had started a pot of canned soup simmering on the fire. "If you need me for anything, I'll be right here."

Sandy didn't understand. Buster didn't think she had to.

"Who's your real wife, anyway?" she asked him. "Me or Whistling Pete? And since when did you start cooking? I've never seen you open a can of beans before."

Buster was wearing one of Estelle's frayed white aprons and scrubbing rusty pans in the sink.

"It's something I've got to do," Buster said. He felt strangely peaceful. "If you love me, you'll try to understand."

"Try to understand," Sandy said. Suddenly, like wind snuffing out a candle, the fight went out of her. "Try to understand."

Buster took his overdue vacation time from the factory

and repaired Whistling Pete's windows and furniture. Every afternoon, after preparing a lunch of chicken broth and fresh fruit salad, he helped Pete out of bed, walked him around the room a few times, and changed the linen. Whistling Pete's body was all slump and desuetude, his complexion jaundiced and scabby. He was losing feathers around his skull and under his armpits.

"We'll get you a nice wool cap," Buster promised one day during their exercise session. "The body loses ninety percent of its heat through the old skull, you know. To keep the body warm, you gotta keep your lid on—get me?"

"That's why we've got gas fires," Pete muttered dreamily. "That's why we've got central heating."

"Go back to sleep," Buster said, laying him back on the cool, fresh sheets. "You don't have anything to worry about for a long, long time."

Usually Whistling Pete drifted off again, but some afternoons, as if driven by the momentum of his own feverish imaginings, he talked out loud in his sleep.

"I dreamed of the white ice," Whistling Pete said. "I was walking south, into a region of thin air and dazzling auroras. Heading into the big nothing, I couldn't stop myself. Not because I wanted to get anywhere specific, but because I couldn't bear to remain where I already was."

The dreams seemed to increase in force and volume, and Buster couldn't decide if this was a good omen. Sitting beside Pete's bed with his newspaper, Buster watched his friend toss and turn with slow intensity, like a kettle heating on a stove. Sometimes he cried or started upright, and Buster soothed him with a steaming wet towel.

"Human beings are the next step," Whistling Pete whispered from time to time. "They'll be here any day now. And if they don't get here pretty soon, then I'm afraid we penguins don't have any choice. We'll have to turn into human beings. You, me, Estelle, Junior, Melody, the girls, the beautiful girls. We'll start erecting supermarkets and shopping malls. We'll drive like maniacs on motorbikes and mopeds. We'll shoot each other in the head, and chew tobacco, and piss on our own front stoops. I have seen the future, Buster, and it is us. Animals who can't stop themselves. Animals who always want more than they've already got."

"It's okay, Pete," Buster said. He shook and repositioned the foam pillows, helping Pete subside back into them. "Stop thinking and relax. It'll be okay, I promise. I'll stick by you. All you've got to do is get better, Pete. And I'll take care of everything until you do."

They buried Whistling Pete beside the pond where he first went fishing with his father. A lid was cut in the ice and Pete's naked body was inserted into the frothy, secret currents, while the attending penguins stood around too stunned, disoriented, or angry to look at one another. On the fringes of the small crowd a few lonely, heavily veiled penguinettes sobbed quietly into black satin handkerchiefs.

When the lid of ice was fitted back into place, a few words were said by each of Pete's surviving relatives. Usually they offered slow, awkward condolences such as "He will be missed" or "He was always a hard worker and good provider," with a dull, casual flourish, as if they were taking turns signing a form letter. The last person to take the mound was Pete's father, who had swum in that morning from his retirement village on The Hobbs Coast. (Pete's mother had died two years previously in a freak skiing accident.)

"Whistling Pete was a good boy," his father said in a cracked, halting voice, trying to read from a sheet of foolscap in his trembling hands. He wore a faded gray flannel shirt, a black wool stocking cap, and wire-rim bifocals. "He was always polite to his parents. He always did well in school, and he always helped his mother with the housework. Now, maybe he exaggerated the truth every once in a while, but that's just the way he was, I guess. He found the truth a little boring, so he tried to embellish it, it was kind of like generosity. Pete always thought big. He was ambitious, and ever since he learned to swim, he dreamed of visiting faraway places and accomplishing great deeds. I remember when he was little, he was such an enthusiastic fisherman. He kept bringing home sacks and sacks of them, more fish than we could possibly eat in one modest household. So then he started giving away the extra fish he caught to poor homes and convalescent hospitals. He always gave that little bit extra to everything he did. Maybe some people considered it selfish. But I always thought he gave life everything he had because he loved it so much."

Mr. Pete paused to wipe a frozen teardrop from one eye and continued in a wet, quavering voice. "Maybe he made some mistakes when he grew older. He never visited his mother and me after we retired, but by then he had a family of his own, so I guess he just got too busy. But he was always good to me and his mother when he was little, and that's, that's . . ."

Abruptly, Mr. Pete began to sob. A hush fell over the mourners. Even some of the succinctly sobbing black-clad penguinettes fell respectfully silent.

Buster stepped up and whispered something in Mr. Pete's ear.

"No, no, I'm okay," Mr. Pete declared irritably and shook his sheet of foolscap at Buster as if he were shooing flies. Then he wiped his glasses with the end of his stocking cap, folded the paper in half, and slipped it into his vest pocket.

"I just wanted to say that Whistling Pete was always polite to his mother and father when he was little, and that's how I'll always remember him."

The Land of the Midnight Sun

Estelle and Junior moved back into the house, and Whistling Pete's father returned to his retirement village by the sea. With much stern ceremony, Buster and Sandy began making what they referred to as "a fresh start." They exchanged small, occasional gifts on personal anniversaries and public holidays, cautiously maintaining a tender, almost obstinate parity.

"No, sweetheart," Buster would demur, leaning to grant her a kiss behind each ear. "This is my night to do the dishes. You washed up two nights in a row last week."

They sat in the living room every evening after dinner sipping Darjeeling, nibbling oven-hot gingerbread, and listening to the BBC World Service. Old empires disintegrating in the Baltic, Adriatic, Sahara, South Africa, Taiwan. Currencies crashing and stock markets rocketing. The pose and strut of presidents, businessmen, pretenders, and kings. "Before civilization," Whistling Pete used to say, "we never had time to realize what we didn't have. Now we've got all the time in the world to worry about what we'll never keep." Sitting with Sandy in the newly redecorated living room, Buster often felt Pete's voice sneak up behind him like a physical presence. It was a summons to attend conversations never conducted, a simple memory of resonance.

In the mornings before work, Buster took long, aimless walks into the wilderness, wrapped tight in his sealskin parkas and scratchy woolen underdrawers. He knew this was the dream Pete had died trying to realize, and that if he tried to realize it himself, then he would have to die, too. Not a dream of comfort or plenitude, but a sort of homeless insufficiency. Buster ascended mountains and forded rivers. He skated across plains of ice and refraction, hopping from one jaggedy landmass to another. Some mornings he arrived late for work, where he received three warnings and one official reprimand. One more tardy report or no-show and he would be fired. No explanations asked.

That night at home, Sandy tried to understand.

"Do you know what you're doing?" she asked. Sandy had lit soft candles and prepared a cheese soufflé. She wore a string of pearls, rubber pedal pushers, and a Dacron shower cap—a combination she knew looked really good on her.

"Not really," Buster said. He sat beside the fireplace and waited. He didn't know what he was waiting for anymore; he only knew it would be here soon. "I try not to worry too much, though. If it happens, it happens. I'll get another job. I'll do the best I can."

"I'll do the shopping tomorrow. Is there anything special you need?"

Buster thought about this for a moment, as if it were an especially tricky parable.

"Not really," he said. "These days it's hard for me to think too much about tomorrow."

The Reflection Once Removed

"**I've got this** idea," Raymond Donahue said, reaching under the dining room table to dislodge Charlotte's Pomeranian from his ankle. "And I've had this idea for quite a while now. Why don't we make it illegal for people to practice psychoanalysis without a license? And I don't just mean in California. Why don't we think about it as a nation*wide* ballot initiative?"

"I'm serious, honey. I really am." Charlotte reappeared from the kitchen, producing more food items that Raymond hated. Beets and tough, sinewy string beans. Gristly chicken loaf and green olives stuffed with a vaguely gelatinous, pimento-like substance. "You've got a womb complex, Raymond; you can't help yourself. It says so right here in this great book I've been reading by Dr. Elliot P. Bernstein."

Charlotte ladled more unrequested string beans onto

his plate. "The womb complex is a complex that afflicts many young men of your background. Young men who were overprotected by their mothers develop low self-esteem motivation factors that cause them to distrust their female cohabitants or lifetime mating partners. They grow insular and self-obsessed. They retreat into private fantasy worlds. They hardly ever take their mating partners out for dinners or dancing and watch an excessive amount of sports events on TV. Eventually they develop a thinly concealed hostility for all women, even their mating partners who love them, since no woman, however loving, can provide the perfect original safety they once enjoyed behind the walls of their mother's womb."

"My mother was a belladonna addict who slept around with bikers," Raymond said distractedly. The Pomeranian, like a homing missile, had latched onto his ankle again, humping even more earnestly. "I was raised by my father in Burlingame."

"It's the same thing," Charlotte said, passing him a suspicious brown plastic bottle emblazoned with thunderbolts and the resounding Liqui-Marg motif. "Honestly, honey, I don't know why you're being so evasive."

Raymond gave the Pomeranian a swift, perfunctory kick, which sent it ricocheting off the leg of the sofa with a tiny yelp.

Charlotte shot Raymond a dire look. Her look said, Isn't that just what I should expect from a man with such a well-defined womb complex!

Raymond was watching something green wobble on a plate across the table. He wasn't wearing his glasses but, for one moment, he could have sworn he saw the green object wobble in his direction.

"That's not Jell-O salad, is it?" Raymond asked warily.

The only edible substance in the entire world that Raymond hated more than gristly chicken loaf was Jell-O salad.

"Yes, it is," Charlotte said coolly. "But I'm afraid you're just going to have to wait for dessert."

"*Getting to Know Your Own Enzymes*, Raymond, is not, as you call it, another *crack*pot book."

Sylvia was wearing her Day-Glo nylon jumpsuit, brown cotton leg warmers, and a yellow terrycloth headband. She had just gotten off her Exercycle in the living room to return to the kitchen and give Raymond another piece of her mind.

"The body, Raymond, just *hap*pens to generate its own language. How do you think the brain communicates with its organs and muscles and so on? By means of its highly complex signaling system—that's how. All Dr. Elliot P. Bernstein is saying, Raymond, is that if the body can talk to itself, then there's no reason *we* can't talk to the body. You know, like open some sort of dialogue between the intellect and the metabolism, the soma and the pneuma, the yin and the yang. I don't think you should just go around calling a creative, highly educated man like Dr. Bernstein a cracker brain, Raymond. The man does have a PhD, you know. The man *did* go to Harvard."

Raymond was standing on a kitchen chair and rummaging in one of Sylvia's highest, deepest storage shelves. He gripped a can of Lucky brand hominy grits under his right armpit, and a box of instant mushroom soup packets under his chin.

"He's got a PhD in education," Raymond said. "I don't know if that qualifies the guy to dispense a lot of mumbo jumbo about hormonal linguistics. Whatever the hell that means."

Sylvia emitted an audible little huff. "How many PhD's have *you* got, Raymond? Why don't you tell me. How many PhD's have *you* got, anyway?"

Raymond replaced the soup and hominy on the storage shelf and looked down at Sylvia. Sylvia's white, slender hands were clenched on her hips. She looked quite pretty, he had to admit.

"Have you got anything to eat around this place? I'm kind of starving."

Raymond climbed down from the chair.

"There's lettuce and tomatoes in the fridge, Raymond." Sylvia's hands began to unclench. "Why don't you fix yourself a nice lettuce and tomato sandwich?"

Raymond blinked myopically around the kitchen at the various glimmering appliances. Then he sat down in the chair and absently examined a loaf of Mama Fiber's Whole Earth Bran Bread.

"I don't really feel like a tomato and lettuce sandwich," Raymond said aimlessly. Suddenly he felt very sad, but he didn't know why. "Actually, I sort of felt like a cheeseburger or something."

Within moments, Raymond heard Sylvia's nice legs pumping fresh mileage onto her Exercycle in the living room.

"And then, of course, there's this whole ozone layer thing, and all the carcinogens in our environment, and all that. Like, I was reading this article in *People* magazine? John Travolta's trying to save all the caribou in Alaska, and the American government, just as you'd expect, isn't lifting one tiny finger to help." Penny showed Raymond the little finger of her left hand. They were standing in the frozen-food aisle at Von's, and Raymond was examining two different brands of frozen zucchini lasagna. After a moment of dull reflection, Raymond replaced them both in the misty frozen-food case.

"It's about time somebody began doing something about these important problems, don't you think?" Penny was peering into the frozen-food case, as if for signs of life. "I mean, too many people have been too me-oriented for too long. Like I've been reading this great book lately called *The Culture Revolution*, by this very famous guy, Dr. Bernstein? He says that me-oriented types of people are the saddest types of people in the entire world, because they're unable to bathe in the cultural vibrations that less self-centered people share with each other all the time. Did you know they sell Dr. Bernstein's excellent book right here in this very supermarket? Well, they do. In fact, it just happens to be number three on the *New York Times* paper-back best-seller list. By the way"—Penny's jeweled fingers tapped at the Bird's Eye Frozen Vegetable Platter Raymond was examining—"what's your name, anyway?"

Raymond replaced the frozen vegetables in the frozen-food cabinet. He had been shopping for an hour now, but no matter how many crowded shelves of food he investigated, all he could think about was the day-old Carl's Western Bacon Cheeseburger he had eaten that morning for breakfast. Raymond's shopping cart contained a loaf of bran bread and a plastic gallon carton of generic 100 percent orange juice.

"My name's Raymond," Raymond said after a while. "And I don't mean to be forward, but according to your friend, Dr. Bernstein, I'm suffering from a pretty severe case of womb complex right now. I should probably warn you about that right off."

Some nights Raymond dreamed about food. Char-broiled steaks, potatoes with sour cream, pot roasts and gravy, breasts of chicken simmering with sweet, translucent juices, spare ribs and pork chops and veal Parmesan and turkey pot pies. Usually he started awake in bed just as he reached for it, as if he had transgressed some ontological boundary.

"What's the matter, honey?" a woman's voice asked.

Raymond could still smell the steaming vegetables, the tender slabs of sirloin and lemony trout. The woman's smooth hand touched his face.

"Where am I?" Raymond asked.

"You're with me. You're at my house."

"What year is it?"

"Nineteen ninety-five."

"How old am I? Where do I work?"

"You're thirty-eight, honey, and no spring chicken. You sell advertising space for California's largest home advertising magazine, *The Bargain Buyer*. Your offices are in Sherman Oaks."

Raymond reached out for the end table and found his cigarettes. His sense of vertigo withdrew with a smooth, sliding sensation.

"What am I doing here?" he asked the woman.

"Not too much, baby. I'm afraid you haven't been doing too much good around here at all."

It was becoming increasingly difficult for Raymond to remember who he was with, how long he had known her, and what exactly she meant to him. Every morning he awoke in strange bedrooms where the quality of light lay strangely distributed across things he did not recognize. Often the bed beside him was empty, and he ventured alone into weirdly gleaming bathrooms where he puzzled at unusual brands of shampoo and deodorant, or scalded himself trying to adjust the complicated, often futuristic-looking shower devices. The women left him microwave-ready meals wrapped in plastic on their immaculate kitchen tables, and hasty notes scrawled on the backs of torn envelopes and advertising leaflets.

Make yourself at home, the notes told him. *Be back soon.*

Raymond uncovered the waiting meals and sniffed at them. Sometimes the food resembled muesli, or a nutty, fibrous substance. Sometimes it resembled humus, tara-masalata, or something with cheese. Vainly Raymond searched through unfamiliar cabinets for cornflakes, Froot Loops, or anything he recognized. Instead he discovered snail pellets and gardening supplies, rusty woks and elaborately packaged fondue kits, unpaid utility bills and neglected pastry. Usually he just burned a piece of bran bread in the toaster, and soothed it with whatever brand of butter substitute he could find in the refrigerator. Breakfasts in strange houses, Raymond thought, were a pretty depressing experience—especially for a man rapidly approaching middle age.

He couldn't remember their names or faces anymore, but only the books they left behind. *Learning to Be and Love Yourself*, *Developing Your Own Me-ness Strategy*; *Eating for a Better IQ*; *Men Who Love Too Much and the Women Who Leave Them*; and, of course, the perennial best seller *Doing It Your Way*, with a special introduction by Frank Sinatra Jr. All of these books were either written by Dr. Elliot P. Bernstein or in collaboration with him, and they featured numerous graphs and charts concerning the relationships between self-esteem and diet, oogenesis and body language, erogenous zones and statewide radon activity. Raymond often caught himself gazing absently at the various diagrams and illustrations for hours while the ice dissolved in his drinks, or his mugs of coffee grew cool on the kitchen table.

Raymond figured that if all the women he had ever known were even half right, then he suffered from a pretty extraordinary range of personal problems that included narcissism, self-doubt, abstract behavior patterns, colitis, diminishing alpha wave activity, various neural and lymphatic disorders, severe overdependencies on alcohol, antibiotics, and TV, and an almost psychotic disregard for the achievements of supply-side economics.

"I don't think I have to tell you, Raymond," a blond woman with a Karmen Ghia once said, "but you're one really screwed-up individual. Don't take it personally or anything. I just thought it was something you ought to know."

In September, Raymond enrolled at the Dr. Bernstein Center for Adjustable Behavioral Abnormalities in Reseda, where for ten days he was subjected to the relentless schedules, strategies, and ministrations of an impressive battery of counselors, psychotherapists, herbalists, dietary technicians, muscular coordinators, adaptive macrosocietal engineers, and one rather impolite old lady who ran the snack bar. The impolite old lady who ran the snack bar was named Eunice, and she wore fluorescent makeup, butterfly glasses on a chain around her neck, and mottled, inadequately dyed hair in a bun. Usually Raymond sat at the snack bar on a stool and drank Mocha-Max, a single-blend coffee and creamer substitute, while he vaguely examined the shelves of heavy-looking carob cookies and vegan soufflés displayed behind glass cases like exhibits in some inedible museum. Eunice never smiled at Raymond even once, and whenever he arrived at the snack bar she emitted long, exasperated sighs, as if Raymond were the most boring man who had ever lived.

"You know, Eunice, I've been thinking," Raymond mused aloud, examining the thin pink residue at the bottom of his depleted mug of Mocha-Max, "do you remember all those women in my life who keep telling me what a self-centered, screwed-up wreck I am? Well, come to think of it, none of those women is what you could actually call perfect. I mean, they're perfectly *nice* and all, but almost without exception they believe in things like reincarnation, alien visitors from outer space controlling the Pentagon, and astrology. Come to think of it, most of them are Capricorns. Do you think that means anything, Eunice? That most of them happen to be Capricorns?"

Whenever Raymond looked up, Eunice began banging dishes in the sink and scrubbing them with a frayed, soapy rag. Raymond had to admit that she was not the most patient and attentive listener he had ever encountered, but at least she found him so boring that she didn't offer him any constructive criticism of her own. Perhaps, Raymond thought, it was because Eunice realized, somewhere deep inside her dim, soapy brain, that if there was one thing Raymond wasn't short of lately it was constructive criticism.

For ten days Raymond was analyzed, steamed, acupunctured, rolfed, screened, vilified, hugged, X-rayed, audited, sensorily deprived, and enrolled in afternoon swimming lessons at the enormous, Olympic-size Dr. Bernstein Swimming Pool, which was in the sweeping, brilliantly scented Dr. Bernstein Botanical Gardens. He was required to chart daily graphs of his heart and metabolic rates, and to keep a secret diary in which he purged himself of his most shameful resentments against the Dr. Bernstein Center and all the highly qualified people there who were just trying to help him.

"People who never learn to swim suffer from womb insecurity neurosis, which is a very difficult form of neurosis to deal with, especially when you're a lady," Bunny told Raymond every afternoon during their daily aqua-therapy session. Meekly, Raymond held his breath while Bunny plunged his head underneath the sparkling, chlorinated water, or trawled him into the deepest part of the pool and held him in a back-float against the thin surface. "For many people, the womb is the only happiness they ever knew. But once they're born, everything goes straight downhill. They become deeply afraid of feeling happy and secure, because they believe such feelings can only lead to suffering and deprivation. This is what we call a bad behavioral syndrome, Raymond. Bad behavioral syndromes are habits you develop that make you unhappier than whatever experiences caused you to develop those habits in the first place. Does that make sense to you, Raymond? Do you realize that people are often their own worst enemies, sometimes without even knowing it?"

Bunny was the most extraordinarily fat woman Raymond had ever seen with most of her clothes off. Her two-piece swimsuit resembled wire bindings on a bale of hay. "When you're a lady and you feel unloved, you find it impossible to love yourself," Bunny told Raymond later at Eunice's snack bar. "So you just sit around your apartment all day, watching television and eating yourself into oblivion. You become massively fat, and the fatter you get, the more unhappy you become. And so you eat more, and get more unhappy. And so on and so forth. Since I met Dr.

Bernstein, I have lost nearly eighty pounds. As a result, I have developed a more assertive attitude toward my own femininity. Now, how does one of those carob cookies look to you, Raymond? I think I wouldn't mind a carob cookie to go along with my Mocha-Max. How about you?"

"I don't think so," Raymond said politely, listening to a bubble of pool water oscillating thinly in his left ear. It sounded like hovering spacecraft in a science fiction movie. "I think I'll just finish my Mocha-Max and go back to my room."

On the day of his release from the Dr. Bernstein Center for Adjustable Behavioral Abnormalities, Raymond whistled Stevie Winwood's "Back in the High Life Again" all the way home. He went directly to Hamburger Hamlet and ordered his favorite meal, the cheesesteak and fries with a large Coke, and strawberry shortcake for dessert. He flirted with all the waitresses, drank three jumbo vodka tonics, and even purchased a pack of Marlboros, which he smoked with self-indulgent dispatch. As far as Raymond was concerned, the best thing about the Dr. Bernstein Center for Adjustable Behavioral Abnormalities was not having to be there anymore. It was like having a malignant brain tumor go into remission, or a merciful governor call just in time to stop the switch from being thrown.

"At first I tried to fight it," Raymond told Wendy, Crystal, Sylvia, and Marie over succeeding evening meals at their houses. "I didn't have enough confidence in myself to trust in the sincere, highly qualified concern of others. I was antisocial, and spent most of my time in my room. Whenever one of my counselors or behavior monitors tried to start up a friendly conversation, I wouldn't even give them the time of day. Then one afternoon while

I was sitting smugly alone in my room, I remembered what Dr. Bernstein said once about the negotiable-me strategy. The negotiable-me strategy often arouses conflictual-action scenarios between itself and the you-negation paradigm. This is the same thing as saying that one's self-vocabulary has become deverbalized in a highly chaotic manner."

With evident concern, Raymond reached across the table and touched Wendy, Sylvia, Crystal, or Marie's hand.

"Are you following what I'm trying to tell you?" Raymond asked. "Or am I using too much technical jargon for you to relate with where I'm at?"

When the various women in his life stopped returning his calls, Raymond gratefully settled into a routine of smooth, uneventful complacency. He subscribed to cable and began taking extended vacation and sick leaves from his office. He bought a window planter for the front porch, and a cherry-red hummingbird feeder for the kitchen window. He ate late breakfasts and watched the hummingbirds dart, hover, and weave outside in the glistening blue air. Whenever the phone rang, it was usually somebody promoting newspapers or magazines, or Bunny from the Dr. Bernstein Center trying to sign him for a "follow-up" session at the new Dr. Bernstein Holiday Self-Actualization Camp in Napa Valley. Raymond wished Bunny all the luck in the world and told her that if he could find time, he would definitely call her back right away. Then he had his telephone disconnected and bought from the pound a small, mottled gray puppy that he named Cylus. For the first few weeks, Cylus went to the bathroom all over Raymond's apartment. Whatever Cylus didn't pee or crap on, he chewed to ribbons with a happy animal patience. Cylus was an amiable, energetic young dog who knew how to enjoy the simple things in life. And when you got right down to it, Raymond thought, the simple things in life were all that really mattered.

Then, one afternoon in late May, someone knocked at the front door. When Raymond opened it, he found himself gazing into the book-jacket-familiar face of Dr. Bernstein, whose smile glinted as cheerily as the thick bifocal lenses of his horn-rimmed glasses.

Looking up from one of Raymond's well-chewed suede cowboy boots, Cylus growled.

"You may be able to run and hide from Dr. Bernstein," Dr. Bernstein said wisely, "but it's not so easy to run and hide from yourself. As I'm sure we all well know."

An automobile horn sounded abruptly in the street. When Raymond looked down at the curb he saw Bunny seated at the driver's wheel of an open-top pink Cadillac convertible. Bunny waved merrily. Pale flesh flapped in her armpit.

It took Raymond a few seconds to regain balance. Then he plunged straight ahead.

"You're absolutely right, Dr. Bernstein," Raymond said. "You're absolutely, abso*lute*ly right."

"Self-motivating behavioral strategies don't start working overnight, Raymond." As Dr. Bernstein entered Raymond's apartment, he gave appreciative nods at the television, video, sofa bed, and CD player. "Behavioral abnormalities often require *years* of cautious, professional assessment. You're a young man with a lot of promise, Raymond. But you're also a young man who is very definitely and very profoundly screwed up. And I wouldn't say such a thing if I didn't truly care about your well-being as an individual."

"I'm sure you wouldn't, Dr. Bernstein." Raymond was

glancing frantically around the living room. "I'm sure you'd never do anything to endanger my happiness and well-being." Raymond systematically noted and disregarded the locations of a Rand McNally atlas, a rabbit-ear television antenna, a hearthtop piggy bank, and some thick-framed museum prints of Picasso, Matisse, and Cézanne.

On the floor, Cylus's growl roughened. He was sitting up and watching Dr. Bernstein. He had forgotten his partially macerated cowboy boot altogether.

"Why don't you throw a few clothes together," Dr. Bernstein said, "just enough for a day or two at the Holiday Camp. You'll also need to bring along some cash. And your checkbook—don't forget your checkbook. Your Visa and MasterCard cards."

"I'll do that," Raymond agreed happily and departed for the back bedroom, where he opened his battered brown overnight bag and filled it with socks, underwear, toothbrush, toothpaste, denim trousers, and denim shirts. Then he went into the closet and, from underneath the moldering laundry, retrieved his notched and yellowing Louisville Slugger baseball bat. He hurried back to the living room.

In the living room Dr. Bernstein was saying, "Nice doggy. This is my nonthreatening, beta-status posture, doggy. Can I pat you? Can we be friends? Ouch!"

Dr. Bernstein took a sudden backward step.

"You brainless little turd!"

Dr. Bernstein was raising his open hand just as Raymond hammered the back of Dr. Bernstein's skull with the Louisville Slugger. Raymond had never been a particularly good baseball player, but it had been his favorite sport anyway. He removed Dr. Bernstein's cash-fat wallet and stuffed it into the vest pocket of his Wrangler jeans jacket. Then he went to the front door and waved at Bunny in her pink Cadillac.

Bunny waved back happily and honked the horn.

Raymond returned to the living room and gave Dr. Bernstein another firm whack with the Louisville Slugger, just for good measure. Then he bundled up Cylus, climbed over the backyard fence, and hailed a cab at Van Nuys Boulevard.

"Not supposed to allow dogs in this cab," the driver told him.

Raymond showed the driver a wad of bills from Dr. Bernstein's wallet.

"LAX," Raymond said. "You better step on it."

The driver contemplated the wad of bills reflected in his rearview mirror. He removed a gray lump of gum from his mouth and placed it in the ashtray.

"Where you headed?" he asked after a while.

"To get my mind straight," Raymond said. "To raise my consciousness. To increase my self-esteem coordinating capabilities in a highly resolute, predetermined manner." Raymond gazed out the window at the smoggy, opaque Los Angeles skyline, the angry cars and drivers, the roaring buses and airplanes. Los Angeles, he thought, had never looked better.

"But this time I'm going to do it in Rio."

Doggy Love

Tall, Dark, and Furry

I find it quite awkward all this silly writing about myself, but here goes.

I am a reasonably attractive mixed-breed setter and blond lab (on my mother's side) seeking a companionable mate in the vicinity of Regent's Park, where my master takes me most afternoons between four and five-thirty. I am three years old and, while still a virgin, my genitalia remain fully intact, which has led to some rather embarrassing confrontations with my master's guests recently. Especially if they've been in contact with a female dog in the last, say, seven or eight hours.

I can't help myself. I'm quite amorous by nature.

I enjoy grooming (myself and others), television (with the sound off), and most of Hayden's late wind concertos, even though they are normally dismissed by the world's dull-as-dishwater Mozart enthusiasts. I'm not disparaging Mozart, understand. I just think there were a lot of equally talented eighteenth-century composers running around Europe, even if their lives weren't melodramatic enough to inspire an Oscar-winning film by Milos Forman.

My ideal partner would be a mixed breed like myself, since I don't want to get into a lot of weird social games about who pisses where. She should be attractive, with a nice rump, and enjoy the same things I do, such as catching flies, and illegally bathing in the duck pond. Also, it would help if her master got along with my master, kind of like in *101 Dalmatians*. My master, incidentally, is a very kind (and totally unattractive) human male who doesn't like living alone any more than I do. When he's not at work flogging surplus capital in the City, he lies around the house masturbating and watching Nazi documentaries on the History Channel.

No time wasters, please. Photo available on request.

This Lady's Not for Stroking

Dear TDF,

I joined this service as a trial member a few nights back when I came across your profile. You sound really nice and yes, I, too, live within the immediate vicinity of Regent's Park.

It feels sad joining a computer dating service, but I'm a middle-aged bitch who has never been on a proper date in her entire life, so I've got to start somewhere.

I should mention right off that I'm not a virgin. This is due to an unfortunate week spent in the so-called "animal-friendly" Doggy-Do Kennels in West 14, when my mistress went to Barbados. It's an experience I'd just as soon not talk about right now.

I hate trying to describe myself, so I've attached a recent e-photo. Sorry my mistress is in it, but she butts into all my photos. And yes, I realize she is pretty unattractive, even for a human female. But she has a good heart and walks me twice a day. So I guess I probably love her.

As for my likes and dislikes, here goes.

I like long runs at the beach; raw meat (though I can get along fine on cereal); and lazy days lying at home on the shag carpet with a good video. I guess it's hard to describe my ideal mate, since it boils down to a matter of chemistry, but I value honesty and a good sense of humor above all else. And well, okay. A great-looking rump doesn't hurt.

On the other hand, I hate phoniness and cynicism and needless cruelty to trees.

Hope to hear from you soon,
Denise

Russian Princess Seeks American Prince

Zdrastvuyte from Mother Russia, where lonely Slavic princess find herself living with great-nippled Mamma and six beautiful lesbian sisters. I am being much fond of America and its people all the time, where I would like to visit shortly, preferring it be in company of tall handsome butch American so-and-so. Perhaps you may find yourself this hunky pup as described?

Perhaps we become pen pals and you help me with my troubled English?

Love,
Anastasia

P.S. My rump not so terrible for looking at neither. But why take my word for it? Check out my doggy action at wolfbitches.co.ru. And prepare yourself for hot humpy loving all night long!

Lovely

Dear Denise,

Thank you so much for your lovely photo. I had my doubts before, but perhaps this Internet dating service has its merits.

Time will tell, perhaps.

Please find attached a recent photo of myself on holiday last spring in the Lake District, a gorgeous country filled with so many brilliant smells you wouldn't believe it. I know I'm no Rin Tin Tin in the looks department, but that has never left me wanting for female admirers, since I possess many compelling natural odors that are not convertible into rich text format.

Of course, this innate attraction to the opposite sex has never paid off in what might be called carnal dividends. Sure, I'm allowed to race and frolic with the ladies of Regent's Park, but once the action gets serious? My master hits me on the nose with a rolled-up copy of *Private Eye*.

I loathe *Private Eye*. I don't know about you, but I genuinely loathe it.

Maybe we could meet sometime soon. My master and I usually arrive at Marylebone Green around four or four-thirty.

Is your mistress persuadable?

Your new friend,
Randall

Do You Yahoo?

Dear Randall,

I'm sorry I took so long getting back to you. My mistress was home sick and I couldn't get near the PC.

What a handsome doggy, Randall; I'm really impressed. You're definitely a lot better looking than you seem to realize. (Not that looks matter to me in the long run.)

Actually, I still have my doubts about this dating service. With the obvious exception of yourself, Randall, the only people who ever write me seem like total creeps and weirdos. Russian pornographers, cosmetic surgeons, international loan brokers, and e-perverts of every species and description. It makes you wonder about the genetic imperative, doesn't it? Reproduce or die. Is that what it's all about?

Being a single female in the big city has made me a little cynical, I guess.

As far as an assignation, I'll see what I can do. There are two ends to every leash, as my old mom use to say.

Love,
Denise

Doggy Doggy Doggy Doggy

Doggy doggy doggy me love doggy doggy are me favorite me like big doggy me like strong mean doggy doggy get mad and bite me doggy get mad and chase me down and bite me hard me like big strong doggy bite me hard miaow sorry for that miaow sorry for that me a big doggy me a strong doggy and want lots of doggy love want lots of mean doggy love miaow sorry sorry big mean doggy paws are too big for master keyboard miaow love the big doggy love the big doggy doggy love me?

Please write back please send photo of big mean doggy growling hot angry all night long photo please jpg format please big doggy so hot and angry me want you so bad me very big doggy me very strong doggy please love me please.

Your obedient doggy need discipline now,
Rosco the Very Big Doggy Definitely Not a Cat Miaow

A Perfect Day

Dear Denise,

What a lovely day in the park. Even if the best part did only last a few seconds.

I love my master and remain devoted to him. But if he ever goes near you again with that rolled-up copy of *Private Eye*, I'll see to it personally that he spends the rest of his life learning to sit on one buttock.

Will write more later but I can already hear his feet on the pavement and smell his awful signature odor wafting through the kitchen window. I can't help myself.

I just start barking like crazy.

Will write more soon,
Randall

Counter-conditioning

Dearest Randall,

What can I say? I detected a pretty convincing whiff from our correspondence, but as soon as I smelled you coming across the children's playground I knew you in my bones, Randall. You make me feel like radar.

It was so perfect. The bits of sun shining through and the green grass and the dusty pollen everywhere. Racing and snapping at each other and then you caught me (just at the moment I let you) and please, don't blame your master for getting strict with that rolled-up rag. We both kind of deserved it.

That weird orange cat freaked me out, though. Slithering through the nasturtiums and peering and hissing and licking himself. What a creepy guy.

Do you think our respective masters hit it off? They hardly looked each other in the eye, which, considering their appalling features, is pretty understandable. And the smell!

How can they make love face to face?

Love,
Denise

Brainy Hunk Seeks Same or Better

As you can see from the attached photo, I'm a great-looking, well-exercised, full-blooded German shepherd who believes in maintaining himself both in body and mind. As such, I spend large parts of the day contemplating life's impenetrable mysteries, such as the meaning of existence, or the corporate destruction of animal life. Not to mention I once caught thirty-seven Frisbees in a row at the beach.

Do you ever wonder what's really going on inside the heads of our bizarre and often useless masters? Do you ever wonder how healthy, intelligent dogs such as ourselves kept in touch before this marvelous invention called the Internet? Do you feel it's time for a revolutionary change in the cause of animal rights? And I'm not just talking about the poor cows and pigs being chopped up for sandwiches. I'm talking about us dogs, who have been unfairly restricted from attending our nation's churches, schools, and government buildings for centuries.

When was the last time you saw a dog run for Congress or Parliament? And considering the woeful state of our Western democracies, who could it hurt?

If you ever stay awake nights worrying about these and other questions, please drop me a line. And don't forget to attach a photo of your hairy posterior, just so I know our chemistry is clicking.

Love,
Rex

So Long You've Been Gone

Denise? Honey?

Every day we go to the park and you're not there. I know it's hopeless in terms of a long-term relationship. I know our masters are too hideous to develop an attachment to one another. But I can only think about tomorrow, Denise. I need to see you.

Even if it's for only an hour or a minute.

Will I? Soon?

Love,
Randall

Someone to Share the Magic

Dear Randall,

Can't talk now. I've been doing a little research and you won't believe what I learned.

I feel so ashamed for all those silly, cynical things I said about Internet dating services!

Hold on, baby. We're almost home.

Love,
Denise

Oriental Beauty Seeks American Male for Much Loving

Do you often wish for lovely Oriental bitch with much loving for to give? Do you live in warm climate with many electrical appliances for personal entertainment and comfort? Do you much desire small bundle of Chinese love to cuddle in your big soft doggy bed? Me would wish enjoy such cozy doggy bed much time soon.

Perhaps you consider marriage or cross-breeding or even cohabitation with little Chinese beauty of much loving to give.

Please send photo of esteemed doggy self along with photo of sunny backyard, photo of local trees and vegetation, photo of master(s) and/or mistress(es), and especially photo of cozy doggy bed.

Me looking forward often to hearing from you much time early.

Love,
Yinyang

First Contact

Dear Reginald of Regent's Park,

Please believe that I never evinced myself in this brash manner previously, but I was browsing the singles Web sites and consequently made visual contact with your photo and profile under the mutually intriguing title "Lonely but Loving." What a fortuitous circumstance of formidable complexity!

Perhaps you will not recall an incident of such inherent triviality, but we actually encountered one another in Regent's Park last week, or more accurately, our canine associates encountered one another in what might have developed into an unwholesome public display had you not intervened with your handy magazine, of which I am likewise fond on many occasions.

I have considered your scent often in the many weeks since our encounter and cannot get your attractive buttocks out of my mind. You will have to pardon my American bravado and vocabulary. I believe you refer to it as your "bum," and might consider it gauche for a strange bitch such as myself to speak of it openly in free correspondence.

Please excuse my American candor, however, and perhaps my resultant awkwardness in formal composition regarding these matters. But I felt I must write you since it has caused me much joy to contemplate our reencounter in a parklike setting of our mutual convenience.

Perhaps I might put this more bluntly. Could we perhaps meet sometime soon? Since you are the male aggressor in such matters, I will leave the time and place to your decision utterly.

Might it not be pleasing to our canine associates to come along for the encounter? I am sure they have learned their lesson, and will not grow excessively amorous in any way disturbing to public decency, especially that of the English.

In case you are lachrymose in recalling my attractivity, I have enclosed an e-photo of my most compelling feature. Please use as you see fit, say as a screen saver on your computer, which would remind you of my charms periodically and will arouse your semen delivery mechanisms.

Being a female of shy and reticent demeanor I have surprised myself fully with this open display of honesty, and ask that you kindly not remind me of such displays in the future, as they might scare me away, or make me less receptive to the types of licking and sniffing I enjoy upon first greeting in an amorous style of behavior.

Please understand that I am not a "loose woman" whatsoever but have spent my entire life saving up my passions for someone who smells exactly like you.

Anticipating your reply,
Candy

Ready for the Adventure?

Dear Denise,

What a brilliant bitch. I can't tell you how proud I am.

Bonehead has been running around all day with his head in the clouds.

He can't sit still for a minute. He even bought me a new collar with these green, gemlike studs in it. They're just colored glass, but I can't wait for you to see how it looks on me.

My master did himself one better. He's had a haircut, a facial, a manicure, and even started using a moisturizer.

He smells as bad as Lysol air freshener, but he has a good heart and I hope your mistress appreciates all the time he's been putting into his appearance. (Not that she's any gift to nature herself, if you ask my opinion.)

I'm so excited I could piss all over the crummy linoleum. But I'm saving everything I have for you!

See you in the park, muchacha!

Love, Randall

Satisfied Customer

Dear Doggylove.com,

My name is [*name withheld*] and I'm writing to thank you so much for your lovely dating service.

I guess I've always been cynical about these deals in the past, but that was before I met [*name withheld*] and found out how wonderful true love can be.

It seems like only weeks ago we were living in our separate domiciles, chewing our crunchy biscuits and moping, with nothing more exciting to look forward to than a scratch behind the ear from one of our sad, homely masters. Then we joined doggylove.com and our lives were transformed into a magical miracle of romance.

Even our masters got in on the act, mated, engendered an offspring, and bought a house in the country, to which we will be transporting our doggy beds in a few short days. Not to mention have a litter of our own and raise them in open harmony with nature, much like in the concluding scenes of our favorite movie, *101 Dalmatians*.

Sometimes I turn to [*name withheld*] in the night and say to him, "Honey, bite me on the rump. I must be dreaming!"

And [*name withheld*] always does exactly what I ask. Because, of course, he truly cares.

Yours sincerely,
Lost in Heaven

Editorial Reply

Dear Lost in Heaven,

Thanks so much for sharing your positive, life-affirming experiences with the rapidly expanding membership of doggylove.com, which has recently opened branches in Germany, the Netherlands, Saudi Arabia, and the Philippines. All over our exciting planet, canines are coming together to share their unique passions for giving and living.

So go out there and get the love you need! Don't settle for second best! Or you'll find yourself lying alone someday in a smelly basement with nothing but a red rubber chew toy to keep you warm.

As our cofounder and senior board member Rosco the Big Mean Doggy likes to say: *Have faith in someone besides yourself, no matter what they tell you, no matter how they smell . . .*

So until next week, happy sniffing to all you hunky dudes and bitches!

Miaow!
(Ooops, stupid keyboard. Let's run by that again.)
Woof woof.
And love don't come truer than that.

Goldilocks Tells All

"I didn't know what I was getting into," Goldy told the crowd of demographically diverse audience participants. "I never thought it would go so far. Imagine yourself in my place, just a kid really, lost in the Enchanted Forest with no familiar paths in sight. Winds howl, owls hoot, the woody noose tightens. When suddenly you smell porridge bubbling in a big iron pot, and after heeding your nose for a mile or so, find it. What looks like salvation. But what turns out to be something a whole lot worse."

Goldy paused long enough to hear the high-ceilinged studio hum.

"Bavarian modern, baby," Goldy continued. "With cotton-candy smoke burbling from a candy-cane-striped chimney, and all the doors wide open. So what would *you* do, ladies? Maybe what I did—climb through one of those convenient, Hobbit-style windows, pull yourself up to the porridge bowl, and after a hardy dose of victuals, fall asleep dreaming of feathery opulence in a just-right lacy bed. I felt like a million bucks. I thought I'd died and gone to heaven. A warm home, warm food, cool sheets, all the things I'd ever dreamed about and more. Little did I realize what was hastening toward me through the hoary woods. Little did I know what Papa Bear had in store for me when *he* got home."

Goldy let the sentence hang.

I am your sister, Goldy's glance affirmed. And I wouldn't say it if I didn't mean it.

"We've all got a Papa Bear in our lives, ladies, even though we may call him by different names. I'm talking about the guy who comes home every night stinking of pretzels and beer, slamming all the kitchen cabinets, enacting his plans for world domination on our soft, life-affirming bodies. Which brings me, not quite so coincidentally, to the subject of my new book."

Goldy held up a bright, laminated glare to the camera. The studio audience blinked.

"It's my latest," Goldy concluded, "my best, and the one that the *New York Times* recently described as 'thrilling, sad, heartbreaking,' and 'packs a huge wallop.' Entitled *The Goldilocks Syndrome*, it's currently available in the lobby at a today-only discount of $21.95. And if you act *now*, I'll sign and date this sucker at no extra charge."

Goldilocks hated book tours. She hated the silent time in chauffeur-driven stretch limos when the cell phone didn't beep. She hated the virtual landscape of acoustically muffled hotel corridors and velour-scented penthouse restaurants. She hated predawn wake-up calls, the hard crack of ice machines in the night, and hasty publicity girls going ballistic over memos. In fact, the only things Goldy *did* appreciate about book tours were room service and movie people. Because both entered and departed her life on perfectly fitted steel casters. And they always made just enough fuss to let her know they really *cared*.

"We love you, Goldy," Sid Croft said. "We love everything about you. We love the way you look, the way you write, even the way you comb your hair. When Barbara and I first read your book, we couldn't help it, we both said, 'Wow!' Isn't that right, Barbara? When we first read Goldy's book, what's the first thing we said to each other?"

Barbara looked up from her blue loose-leaf notebook and finished biting the eraser off her pencil.

"I'm not sure, Sid. But didn't we both say something like, I don't know. Like 'Wow!'?"

Barbara looked like she had spent most of her life on an IV drip. The only weight and buoyancy in her entire body were confined to her pointy breast implants.

"That's it! That's *it!*" Sid was bouncing up and down on the flexible toes of his beige penny loafers, as if preparing to return a particularly wicked volley. "We said, 'Wow!' We said '*Double* wow!' And what's more, Goldy—we meant every word of it."

Goldy was perched in front of her vanity mirror, gauging the depth of her own reflection. Goldy loved moments like this. Moments when everybody waited for *her*.

"So what is it, Sid?" she asked finally, applying a modicum of blush to each cheek. "I've got a conference call at five and a TV gig at five-thirty."

Sid was as short, round, and immovable as a mailbox.

With an almost audible pop, a bright bead of sweat broke from his receding forehead and slalomed down the side of his face.

"We love the anti-male thing," Sid said, exchanging a rapid semaphore of glances with Barbara. "We love the woman-striking-out-on-her-own thing. And we're really *intrigued* by the three bears in the gingerbread house thing, but maybe we can talk about that, okay? I mean, couldn't they be reindeer, or lions, or even East Germans? Think about it, Goldy. I've got Cate Blanchett's agent on the line, and he just doesn't go for this *bear* thing at all."

Goldy's unmascaraed eyes pinned Sid's reflection to the mirror like a butterfly to a killing tray.

"So what are we talking about, Sid? Because if we're not talking contract, I've got places I'd rather be."

Ahh, Sid thought. Take a deep breath. Now another. This is the moment when Goldy waits for *you*.

Sid reached into the left breast pocket of his white linen sports jacket, withdrew the folded legal documents, and slapped them down on Goldy's vanity table like a summons.

"Of course we're talking contracts, babe. Guild deal, pay or play, megapoints, your script until you lose it. But not until you've gotten us signed releases from all three bears, especially Papa. We're asking primary rights, sub-sidiary rights, foreign rights, you name it. Those bears don't go to the toilet we don't own the rights to it, dig? You deliver what we need, Goldy, and we're gonna make heap-um big medicine on this one. We're gonna make the deal you've been waiting for all your life."

Even Papa Bear couldn't remember what had really hap-pened anymore. He had rationalized events in his mind, and rerationalized them, and rererationalized them. He told Mama Bear one version of events, Baby Bear another, and himself alone in his bed at night still another. He woke from cold sweats dreaming about what might have happened. What probably didn't happen. What never happened but seemed like it had. The most frightening thing of all, though, was that he couldn't escape one firm, unalterable version of his own history. And that, of course, was Goldy's version—available in trade paper, CD-ROM, and audiocassette.

"You ruined the best years of my life!" Goldy screamed, appearing from her long, sleek limousine in a thigh-length sable coat, pearl droop earrings, and a sequined raw silk blouse from agnes b. "And maybe if you hadn't made me lose so much confidence in myself, I could've developed into a more stable, nurturing-type personality. I might've gotten married and raised my own family instead of ending up like *this*. You know what I mean, Papa Bear. Totally fucked up!"

"Why don't you calm down, Goldy," Papa Bear said without inflection. "Then maybe we could talk things over without getting so, you know. Emotional all the time."

Mama Bear stood in the kitchen doorway, wiping her sudsy paws on the hem of her white cotton apron.

Oh, Papa Bear, she thought simply, when will you learn to keep your big mouth shut?

It began as less than a whisper. And ended as more than a roar.

"Me?" Goldilocks replied. "You want *me* to stop being *emotional?*"

As Goldy's heat gathered, Papa Bear gazed out the frosty window at the limo in the driveway. Its density belongs to a different world than this one, Papa Bear thought. Somewhere cleaner, with firmer lines and harder surfaces.

"You *ruin* my life and I'm not supposed to get *hysterical*? You chase me out of my adopted *home* at the most vulnerable age for a young woman, and I'm not supposed to be *hostile*? What kind of animal are you, Papa Bear? Don't you ever think about anybody but *yourself*? "

Giving under the weight of an exclamatory little stamp, Goldy's left stiletto broke with a resounding crack. She staggered but, as per usual, didn't fall.

"You bastard!" she shouted at Papa Bear. "You hairy, honey-sucking *bastard*!"

The words didn't make an impact so much as clear a space in the room. Then, from the upstairs landing, Papa Bear heard it, a soft, assembling presence, like rain gathering behind dark clouds. Footsteps, a slamming door, an aimless cry in the dark.

"I can't stand it! I can't stand it anymore!" Baby Bear screamed from the summit of the stairs. He was wearing his sloppiest Varsity sweat suit and a pair of buzzing stereo headphones. As he pounded the floorboards with his hairy adolescent feet, lamps toppled from tables, and windows rattled in frames.

"All I ever hear about is *you you you*!" Baby Bear cried. "But what about *my* feelings? Why doesn't anybody stop for a minute to think about *me*?"

When things settled down, Mama Bear fixed porridge for everybody. Hot and lumpy for Papa Bear. Tepid and slightly mushy for herself. And in between for Baby Bear and Goldy who, like all good children, preferred to drive straight down the middle of roads so they didn't veer too dangerously toward either side.

"You can sleep in your old room," Mama Bear bossed abstractly as she pottered at the sink. "And Baby can sleep on the convertible sofa in the den. It'll be just like old times, won't it? Goldy and her three bears. Arguing about every little thing, but living their lives the way they're supposed to. Happily ever after for all time."

Goldy dipped steadily into her porridge with the just-right-size silver teaspoon. Meanwhile, Baby Bear sniffled into his checkered linen napkin and kept close tabs on how much of *his* porridge was being eaten by *her*.

"I'm telling you, Sid," the chauffeur said discretely into the hall phone, "take a left on Enchanted Forest Boulevard and drive straight past Seven-Eleven. If you don't believe me, come see for yourself."

It's all so futile, Papa Bear thought. All four of them sitting around the table like old times, nursing their private hurts and grudges, learning a lot of complicated ways not to tell each other anything.

Papa Bear felt it blossom in the pit of his stomach. So much for so long. He couldn't stand to hold it back another minute.

So Papa Bear *roared*.

Causing everybody to jump at least three feet higher than their chairs.

Except Goldy, of course, who stared directly into Papa Bear's eyes and smiled.

"I knew it," Goldy said. "I knew he'd start shouting. When Papa Bear can't persuade people by means of superior reason, he threatens them instead. It's just the sort of dick thing that really makes me puke."

But I'm the one who's scared, Papa Bear thought. And I don't know any way to tell you but this.

"We gave you a bed to sleep in," Papa Bear pleaded.

"We gave you food to eat and clothes to wear. And believe me, I *tried* to be patient and put up with your endless, constant complaining. 'This cereal is too cold,' or 'This bed is too hard,' or 'You can't have red wine with fish— whatever happened to that nice little Chablis Papa Bear was saving in the cellar?' I *tried* to be a good foster father, but okay, maybe I didn't do a very good job. Eventually I couldn't take it anymore. I chased you into the dark woods and you never came back. Jesus, Goldy, I'm sorry, I really am. I'm sick about it nearly every night. Please, Goldy. I'm begging you. Help me make amends."

As Papa Bear talked, Goldilocks grew out of breath, as if she were performing a weird act of ventriloquism. She stood with her tiny fists planted on her overgrown hips, her large, round face flushed and damp.

"You want to make it up to me, Papa Bear? You want to make everything all right?"

Papa Bear breathed silently for a moment.

"Yes, Goldy," he said softly. "I'll do anything. Anything I can."

Goldilocks permitted her frozen expression to lapse into an equally frozen smile. Then she removed the tidy white rectangle of legal documents from her purse and showed them to Papa Bear the way she might show a fly swatter to a fly.

"Well," she concluded, "let's see if we can think of something. Okay?"

"There may not be any third acts in American lives!" Sid Croft shouted through an old-fashioned plastic megaphone. "But there sure as hell are third acts in a Sid Croft motion picture! Let's work together, everybody! And roll on three!"

Papa Bear was so exhausted it felt like a catharsis. Seated in his recliner with a bottle of Weiss Bier braced between his thighs, he let Mama Bear mop his feverish brow with an ice-cool dishcloth.

"One!" Sid Croft shouted. Technicians and administrative assistants went scurrying. The high, hot lights activated with a flash. "Two!"

Jumping her cue, Goldilocks charged out of her dressing room.

"Where's that bitch from Continuity?" Goldilocks shouted, frantic with black eyeliner. Artificial beauty spots were popping off her face like buttons from an overextended blouse. "I asked for forty-one minor changes to this scene and I've only counted seven so far! Don't you guys understand dramatic development? I can't go chasing after Papa Bear! Papa Bear's got to come chasing after *me*!"

On shooting days, Papa Bear didn't know why he bothered. Four months ago he had happily signed away every legal right to his life story just to get Goldy off his back. Now, as a result of those same concessions, it was beginning to look like she would never leave.

"I'm starting over again, folks!" Climbing atop the exhausted luncheon cart, Sid stood among the pink shell shards of king crab and jumbo shrimp like a height-challenged swashbuckler. "And *you*, young lady! I'm talking to *you*, right?"

Sid Croft pointed directly at Goldy. All around her, studio technicians (especially the male ones) started to snicker.

"*You* take another look at your contract. And do it with a good lawyer, okay?"

Papa Bear retreated into a slow shrug. He felt, as usual, unbearably alone.

And, as usual, he was wrong.

"First we live our lives," Mama Bear whispered, "then we get on to the equally hard job of making those lives make sense. We eat jam, drink coffee, belch, defecate, bump our heads in the night, make love, eat more jam, suffer toothaches and bad faith. Then we wake up the next morning and tell stories about what we think happened. We call our friends on the phone. We write letters and compose poorly punctuated e-mail. We publish books, outline screenplays, adopt the latest word-processing equipment, and dream our way through a hundred hibernal lapses. All I'm saying, Papa, is that maybe you and Goldy aren't so different after all. She needs her anger and you need your guilt. Where would you be without each other, huh?"

Mama Bear was showing Papa Bear his chalk mark on the polished wooden floor. Then she brushed lint from his hairy chest with a soft, gray brush.

"One!" Sid Croft shouted.

"I'm ready!" Goldy volleyed back, pulling her ringletted blond wig into place and readjusting her bosom. "Just hold your horses, Sid. I'm *ready*!"

"Two!"

Out of the corner of his eye, Papa Bear spotted Baby Bear at the cappuccino bar, stroking the script girl's pale cheek with tender ursine restraint.

Look, I may be a bear, the stroke implied. And you may be a woman. But that doesn't mean we can't still be friends.

"Three! And that's *action*, ladies! Roll 'em! I got an early date!"

Papa Bear felt the room dilate to the glossy thickness

of a six-inch lens. At which point Goldilocks, with a stamp of her high heels on the parquet linoleum, entered stage right.

"Now, let me tell *you* something, Papa Bear! Nothing you say or do can ever hurt me, because I love myself too much to let you beat me down. Before I'll let your negative-sounding criticisms damage my self-image factor, I'm leaving the Enchanted Forest and never coming back! You can't evict me from your miserable hovel, Papa Bear, because I'm *outta here*!"

Papa Bear took a deep breath, awaiting his cue. And saw Mama Bear in the wings make a perfect round O of her lips.

"O Goldilocks," Papa Bear woodenly pronounced in camera two's general direction, "I stand naked before you in all my testosterone-drenched male rage. My futile penile egocentrism withers in the all-embracing light of your heterogeneous female multiplicity. Forgive me, O Goldilocks, for the terrible indignities your brave female self has suffered in my cruel clutches! What I'm trying to say is that you win, all-powerful woman! You win, you win, you win, you *win*!"

Papa Bear dropped his chin to his chest. It was the closest he could bring himself to self-abasement.

"Cut!" Sid Croft shouted. "And that's a wrap! Let's all work together again real soon!"

Papa Bear waited on his mark for what seemed like forever.

"Let's go, girls," Goldy told Hair and Makeup. "I'm opening a factory outlet in Reseda at six."

Papa Bear watched the overhead arc lights flicker and diminish with a series of foggy pops, while stagehands coiled thick black cables around their burly forearms. Papa Bear could smell her scent and perspiration coming toward him. This was the lie he had been waiting for all day.

"You were wonderful, sweetheart," Mama Bear whispered as the studio lights dimmed. "Maybe Goldy had the best lines. But you definitely stole the show."

Queen of the Apocalypse

Harriet Owen spent her youth making love to other women's husbands. She spotted them in supermarkets and shopping plazas and provided them quick opportunities to introduce themselves while their wives weren't around. Eventually there occurred brief lapses into soft words, too many margaritas and cigarettes, crying over telephones, sex in elevators. Then, as abruptly as recognition, the harried men went away again. Disconnected their office telephones and sent Harriet personal checks in the mail. For Harriet, affairs with married men were a sort of clock. Whirr, tock, tick. They kept Harriet informed about what had just happened in her life and what would happen next.

Hardness was no stranger to Harriet; neither was remorse. "You're not a good girl," her mother often told her. "You are not loving, or honest, or true. You never help with the housework, or care how I'm feeling. And you won't even go to the store or help with the dishes unless I ask." Sometimes Harriet's mother would disappear for weeks at a time, returning with an ostentatious clatter of keys in the middle of the night, a bag of groceries under one arm, a six-pack of beer under the other. And one way or another, it always seemed to be Harriet's turn to cook breakfast. Harriet never understood how it worked out that way, but it always did.

Harriet's mother liked to say that she had been an abstract expressionist long before being an abstract expressionist became popular. All day long she smoked marijuana out of a corncob pipe and wore a loose-fitting terrycloth bathrobe, gazing blurrily at her uncompleted projects leaning against the high, whitewashed walls as if she couldn't tell them apart. Their studio contained two mattresses, three splintering wooden benches, enormous rolls of medium-grain canvas, several knock-kneed stepladders, and countless rusty, splattered paint cans stacked in weird configurations—as if someone, somewhere, secretly intended them to mean something.

Harriet left home when she was seventeen, moved to North Hollywood, and spent every night sitting on the floor of her unfurnished apartment gazing at the palms of her hands as if they were her mother's paintings on a wall. She didn't want to be plain old know-nothing Harriet anymore; she wanted to be better, wiser, and filled with more meaning than herself. "You can't see beyond the world you live in, which is why you will always be sad," her mother used to tell her. "There are those who can grasp the ungraspable and glimpse the unglimpsable, transgressing the world's boundaries on practically a daily basis. And then there are others, like yourself, Harriet, who are afraid to get up and walk through the dark, even across the hall to go to the bathroom. You'll never explore the unknowable, or know anything in the entire world but yourself; there's nothing you can do about it, so don't even try. Now stop crying, Harriet, and please go to sleep. For breakfast tomorrow I want sausage, English muffins, and some of those really cheesy scrambled eggs of yours. I don't know who taught you how to cook those cheesy eggs of yours, Harriet, but it sure as hell wasn't me."

Some nights, when she couldn't sleep, Harriet clipped at blue veins in her wrist with a pair of dull scissors until the blood came. She did things to her toenails with matches and cauterized sewing needles. She gripped metal table knives and inserted them into the sudden frisson of bulb-less lamps and open sockets. This, Harriet wanted to remind herself, was pain and attention. This was what happened when you were bad. A remote bright sensation of inflexibility and heat. A sort of visceral information. When Harriet felt pain, she didn't feel lost anymore, she knew exactly where she was. She felt a world out there trying to hold her. She knew that something existed besides herself.

Every night, just before she fell asleep, Harriet tried to imagine the total destruction of her own body. Flames would work, missiles or bombs. Stroke, angina, renal failure, poison in the bloodstream, plutonium in the water. Suns and planets might explode and take civilizations with them, or the dollar might collapse until Americans couldn't buy bread. Comets would arrive in the night just like prophecies, and then the entire world would know. When the body died, the mind went somewhere else, escaped the embrace of skin and politics and metal. Continents grew infirm, galaxies milky, teeth loose, philosophies abstract. If you were lucky and didn't struggle, you might learn the pain that really mattered. You might learn to be good and survive the memory of your mother. You might finally understand.

Sometimes the bleeding wouldn't stop and Harriet visited the doctor.

"Do you do this to yourself?" he asked. He stood over her during the examination, exerting force and profession. "Or was it some boyfriend? Is it something you ask them to do, or do they just do it anyway?"

"I'm clumsy," Harriet said, closing her eyes, seeing the white, starry impact she saw whenever she contemplated herself. "It happens when I'm cooking at the stove, or chopping vegetables at the sink."

Sometimes the doctors sat behind their desks and watched from far away. They stopped looking at her body. They tried to see into another part of her entirely.

"Why do you do it?"

"*I* don't really do it."

"Is it because you don't like yourself?"

"I like myself fine."

"Have you ever been on medication? Have you ever visited a therapist?"

"I've consulted several therapists," Harriet said. "But I've never taken any prescribed medication."

Then one day a man came along and tried to save her, a man Harriet consequently never forgave nor forgot. Boyd Thomas left his wife and children, changed his job, and moved into Harriet's apartment on Super Bowl Sunday, setting up a provisional base camp on the living room sofa. Every day he went out for groceries and supplies from the local market; he did the chores, washed the dishes, and emptied the trash. Every evening he prepared large, nutritious dinner salads and vegetarian pastas in Harriet's underequipped kitchen and never made a fuss when Harriet refused to eat them. It was a type of cruelty Harriet had never known before. A man who wanted to take care of her. A man who wouldn't go away.

Boyd assembled his dense, secret ministry of affection in Harriet's life while Harriet wasn't looking: new dishes, silverware, appliances, furniture, vitamins, consolation, and advice. Some mornings Harriet awoke to discover new curtains in the kitchen, tools and a workbench in the basement, Boyd's shoes under the bed. "You need to get out more," Boyd told her, arranging the dull clatter of tea things on an aluminum tray. "You need to stop feeling so sorry for yourself. Reenroll in school, for chrissakes. Career management, I was thinking. And please, Harriet, *look* at me when I'm talking to you. Why can't you ever *look* at me? All I ever try to do is what's best for you, and the way you act? It's like I'm not even here."

Boyd intercepted flying plates and glasses with ease, replacing them patiently on shelves where Harriet could reach them again. He entertained crude slurs about his manhood with an attitude of benign and sinister avowal. He took all the sharp objects from Harriet's apartment and destroyed all the matches and solemnly refused to slap her whenever she slapped him. There didn't seem to be anything Harriet could do about it. Wherever she turned, there was Boyd trying to love her. Boyd, with a cold washcloth to wipe her brow. Boyd, with two strong arms to hold her.

In bed at night Boyd stroked her white back with his rasped, knuckly fingers, whispering endearments as if he were pushing bulbs into the dark earth. "I love you," he whispered over and over again, a litany as thick as his embrace, his voice reaching into places even Harriet couldn't go. "You're a really lovely, intelligent woman who deserves the best life has to offer. You shouldn't hate yourself so much; you shouldn't feel so insecure. You're a really special, caring sort of person, and that's why I really, really love and respect you. I want you to be happy. I want to do everything you ever wanted a man to do and more."

Eventually Harriet let Boyd make love to her; it gave her distance and dimension back; it quieted him down. Boyd and Harriet, him and her, man and woman, hammer and earth. She would close her eyes and drift away into the wash of galaxies that wouldn't last, into the casual obliteration of planets that never mattered. Boyd would climb off her; he would hold her in his arms. Something was always gripping at you, whether you wanted it to or not. It might as well be Boyd, she thought, falling asleep, regaining her dreams of catastrophe and annihilation. It was the only submission she could make anymore.

He took her to meet his family—Wanda, Phil, Jane, and Eddy. Wanda and Phil were his parents, Jane and Eddy were his father's children by a previous marriage. "You seem like a really terrific young girl," Phil said. "Boyd has told us so many wonderful things about you. But in all his many wonderful descriptions, he never gave us any idea how pretty you are. Such a pretty, pretty, really pretty girl." They were sitting on the splintery veranda, drinking sun tea spiced with licorice, watching the sunset expand over Hermosa Beach. Phil turned to Wanda. "She really *is* pretty, don't you think? Like in pretty-as-a-picture sort of pretty. Especially her hair."

"Not only that," Wanda said, "but just look at her teeth. I wish I had teeth like that. I could eat anything I wanted."

"And such a nice figure," Phil said, looking her up and down. Phil was a jeweler in Santa Monica. "Boyd must be the envy of all his friends." Phil winked at Harriet and blushed, holding his bony knees together.

"We sure like her better than Marjorie," Jane and Eddy called from the living room, where they basked in the pale, unearthly light of the RCA television. "No matter how nice she pretended to be, Marjorie was always a big, fat drag."

Wanda distributed more tea and packaged cookies. She leaned toward Harriet and stage-whispered, "Boyd's last wife was a very nice woman and provided Boyd's children with a wonderful role model and all that. But she was never a very sexual sort of person. And Boyd, as you must know by now, likes to exchange a lot of good, healthy pleasure with his women. Much like his father, I guess."

Wanda showed Harriet lumpy, granulated sugar in a white ceramic bowl.

"I forget already. Do you take sugar?"

"No," Harriet said. "I never take sugar in my tea."

"She's watching her figure," Phil said. His flushed, vein-burst face winked constantly at Harriet, like a broken signal at a railway crossing. "She doesn't want to lose her gorgeous figure. And neither do we, eh, son? Neither do we."

Boyd married her and bought a house. That was the end, really. There was nowhere left to go.

"It's got a basement and an attic," Boyd said proudly. "Two bedrooms and a den. The kitchen needs work, but there's no problem with heating. And the yard is enormous. Like ten normal-sized yards, really. A big, I mean a really *big* yard. We could have twelve kids running around in a yard like that. They wouldn't see each other for weeks."

The house was wide, complicated, and dense, poured into the earth with concrete, hammered together with wood and nails. Harriet couldn't cry and couldn't sleep, lying in bed all day until Boyd returned home from his subcontractor's job at the mall. She heard the power lines in the street, pigeons on the rooftop, the aluminum rustle of gas in the stove. Every morning cartons of fresh milk appeared on the doorstep. Newspapers, shopping coupons, stray cats howling at the wind.

She bound her feet with twine to cut off the circulation. She plucked hairs from her face and secretly bit her tongue. She ate too many grapefruit and rinsed the cold sores in her mouth with vinegar, salt, and lime concentrate. She explored those areas of her body where sewing needles didn't leave marks. It might be Boyd's house, but it was still her body. I, Harriet told herself, am completely *my* decision.

Boyd began exhibiting a strange and unhealthy concern for Harriet's menses, circling dates on the Val's Used Autos calendar with a black felt laundry marker. "Monday, Tuesday, Wednesday, *Thurs*day," Boyd told himself out loud and circled the final date with a proud little flourish, as if he were endorsing a check to Famine Relief. Then he took the thermometer from the bathroom cabinet, swabbed it with alcohol, and called out Harriet's name.

There was something implacable about the way Boyd made love to her now, as if he were straining against the skin of a bubble, trying to tell her something language could not convey. "I've reinsulated the attic," Boyd told her in bed, rocking gently against her, as cautious as if he were caressing helium. "I've discussed the basement plumbing with a regional contractor. This spring, I'll paint the place. I'll put down new carpets and grass. Depreciation, baby. That's what buries you. By the way, did I tell you I love you, Harriet? Did I tell you you're the most beautiful woman I've ever seen in my life?"

There were books on the bureau beside the thermometer. *The Home Pregnancy Handbook*, *Fertility and Nutrition*, *Conception and the Stars*.

"I don't care if it's a boy or a girl," Boyd often said. "I just hope it's a Gemini. Then everything will be all right."

Harriet felt so estranged from her own body that she couldn't believe it was happening. Nurses; obstetricians; waxy fluorescent corridors; hurrying orderlies; and drugged, dozing patients on gurneys. From the moment the doctor told her, Harriet pretended to play along.

"Get plenty of rest," the doctor told her. "And exercise. A brisk walk every morning should do it. Don't drink to excess, but a little wine in the evening never hurt anybody."

"Okay," Harriet said. She was looking at a dietary chart the doctor had presented her. The chart was printed on an embossed sheet of plastic and depicted colorful pie graphs, statistical charts, and a brief illustrated history of gestation. "I can do that."

"She looks like a Madonna," Boyd's mother said. "She looks like the most beautiful mother-to-be in the entire world." Wanda and Phil arrived every Saturday afternoon bearing homemade soup, casseroles, Tupperware-clad fruit salads, and bright packaged gifts for Harriet to open. Blankets, diaper bags, Nerf toys, music boxes, Pooh books, illustrated nursery rhymes. Harriet tried to look nonplussed.

"She seems so peaceful. So content with herself."

"Her body generates this drug that helps her relax. I read about it once in a magazine."

"She used to be so edgy and insecure. Boyd's been really good for her. He knew all along she just needed someone to care for. It's a woman's biological role. Even when women aren't having babies, they dream about them all the time."

"That's the full flush of motherhood, all right," Phil said wisely and showed Boyd a roll of floral-pattern linoleum for the family room. "And we know it'll be a beautiful baby, because *all* Boyd's women have beautiful babies."

Now every night it was Harriet who wanted to make love, and Harriet who wanted to hold Boyd. Boyd was always reading—*You and Your Baby, Dr. Spock's Guide to Infant Growth and Development, Owning Your Own Home, Building Your Own Bomb Shelter.* He ate Butterfinger candy bars, drank warm beer from aluminum cans, and watched war movies on late-night TV.

"Tell me," Harriet insisted. "Tell me, tell me." Straining against Boyd's density, steel and concrete and brick.

"We have to be careful," Boyd whispered, overturning his paperback on the end table, lowering himself under the blankets as if he were immersing himself in a cold tub. "Your condition. This trimester. For all concerned. You know I love you."

"Tell me," Harriet said, pushing, reaching, clenching his callused hands against her breasts.

"You're going to hurt yourself, honey. Please let me go."

"Tell me, tell me, tell me," Harriet said over and over again, trying to engage the secret harmony of it, trying to make her own words matter again.

"Tell you what, Harriet? What is it you need to know? Tell me what you want me to say and I'll say it. I want to do what you want me to do, Harriet. All I ever wanted to do was that."

One night in early March Harriet awoke and discovered herself suddenly enormous. The sheets and blankets were soaking, wrapped around her sore, swollen thighs like the leaves of a gigantic cabbage. She felt surfeited and overindulged, washed up drunk on a beach somewhere, entangled with rubbery brown polyps and plankton. She reached for the bedside lamp and knocked cake tins onto the floor, empty ice-cream containers and cookie packets. She tried to sit up and failed. Then again, on the count of three. She peeled damp sheets from her legs. Suddenly she was sitting up. She was sitting on the edge of the bed.

Silver shapes glided around the bedroom, as if the moon were riding a carousel. She looked through the gauzy drapes at the freeway, headlights swirling past, an entire universe filled with history and intention. She knew it before she heard it, like the shape of an extracted tooth, intimate and strange.

Somewhere deep inside the house the voice said:

Here we go. It's time.

"I know," Harriet said. "You don't have to tell me. I already know."

Boyd was getting out of bed, already wearing his Levi's and pulling on a blue T-shirt.

"Just relax and stay calm," Boyd said, guiding her

down the front stairs, dispensing an aroma of Old Spice and Vaseline. Their car was idling in the driveway, a '55 Chevy Custom Chief with whitewall tires and padded dash. It was filled with animal patience, like something in a cave.

Then Harriet was in the car. Boyd adjusted her seat and pulled a small, perforated wool blanket across her knees. She watched her fat, freckled hands in her lap.

The voice said, We'll be there in a few minutes; try to relax; this is what you've been waiting for. Pretty soon, everything you ever wanted will be yours.

"Is it really?" Harriet asked. Boyd was slamming the trunk and wiping the rear windshield with a soggy paper towel. "Is this what I've been waiting for?"

Boyd climbed into the driver's seat and slammed shut his door. The automobile was intact now, a perfect bubble of space and heat. The automobile started to move.

"I've been through this before," Boyd assured her. Mist thickened on the windshield, and Boyd activated the wipers. "A piece of cake, really. It's all in the breathing. My first wife, Betty, she panicked, couldn't breathe. Then they injected her with a sedative, and bang! As soon as she stopped thinking, she *breathed*."

They were passing through streets lined with over-turned garbage cans. City lights were everywhere. They just didn't reveal anything.

"Why didn't you tell me before?" Harriet asked. "Why did I have to wait so long to find out?"

"I'm sorry, babe." Boyd was gazing abstractly out the window, computing logistics, distance, road conditions, those soft rear tires that needed replacing. "Why didn't I tell you what?"

"Can I ask questions?" Harriet asked the smooth white

lights wheeling through the car. "Or am I just supposed to listen?"

The hospital was surrounded by brightly illuminated gray parking lots, like some neglected drive-in movie. The doors to the emergency room opened automatically, and Boyd helped Harriet into a wheelchair.

"I called ahead," Boyd told her, "and alerted Dr. Wilde. Don't be frightened. If you need anything, just ask."

There was something in the silence behind Boyd's voice that Harriet needed to hear.

And then, with a long, sustained gasp, Harriet felt her body start to breathe.

"Je-*sus*," Harriet said. "Je-*sus*."

Everything sped up. Harriet was conveyed down long corridors and transferred to a tissue-lined examination table. She reached out. She was holding someone. She pulled the hands closer, closer.

"Tell me," she said. "Tell me, tell me."

"It's okay, baby. They've gone for the doctor. Looks like you're not going to make us wait around, are you? I've told them to give you something for the pain."

The entire room clenched around her. "No," Harriet told him, "no, don't, no, no," without even listening, without trying to decipher what Boyd's words meant.

Then she felt two enormous hands come down, grip her waist, and lift her off the table.

"Je-*sus*," she said. "Je-*sus*."

Her body seemed very far away. She was connected to her own sensations by a long, microscopic filament of light.

"Tell me," she said. "Tell me, tell me, tell me, tell me."

"Tell you what, honey? You keep asking that. Tell you what?"

"Don't," Harriet told his hands. She was trying to

reach into the light's white canvas, the pure, white, soundless texture that once filled her mother's apartment with everything that wasn't Harriet. She thought she saw Boyd but it wasn't him, wasn't him, because Boyd didn't matter, Boyd had never really *been*. Then she saw him, the man with the voice looking down at her, understanding how she felt and what she needed, loving her for all the right reasons. She could see him but she couldn't see him. He was there and he wasn't there.

It doesn't make things any easier, the voice told her. Even when you know, it doesn't make you happy.

"I understand," Harriet said, "it doesn't matter, I don't need to be happy, tell me, tell me, I really *will* understand." Harriet was crying. Exultation filled her with heat and oxygen and light. "This," Harriet cried, "is just *perfect*," and then the hands came down again and struck iron through her stomach, her pelvis and spine and lifted, lifted her off the table, up through the wide, bright air and soft, impactless white glare of the ceiling. Nobody ever told her, but now she knew. She was hurtling through the white air, the bellows of her lungs beating and swallowing at the rough, pale atmosphere like an engine, and nobody had to tell her anything ever again because finally she knew, she knew, she knew, she knew.

The Devil Disinvests

"I don't think of it as laying off workers," the Devil told his chief executive officer, Punky Wilkenfeld, a large, round man with bloodshot eyes and wobbly knees. "I think of it as downsizing to a more user-friendly mode of production. I guess what I'm saying, Punky, is that we can't spend all eternity thinking about the bottom line. Eventually it comes time to kick back, reflect on our achievements, and start enjoying some of that well-deserved R&R we've promised ourselves for so long."

As always, the Devil tried to be kind. But this didn't prevent his long-devoted subordinate from weeping copiously into his worsted vest.

"What will I *do*?" Punky asked himself over and over again. "Where will I *go*? All this time I thought you loved me because I was really, really evil. Now I realize you only kept me around because, oh, God. For you it was just, it was just *business*."

The Devil folded his long, forked tail into his belt and checked himself out in the wall-size vanity mirror. He was wearing a snappy, handmade suit by Vuiton, gleaming cordovan leather shoes, and prescription Ray Bans. The Devil had long maintained that it wasn't enough to *be* good at what you did. You had to *look* good doing it.

Roger "Punky" Wilkenfeld lay drooped over the edge of the Devil's desk like a very old gardenia. The Devil couldn't help it. He really loved this guy.

"What can I tell you, Roger?" the Devil said as reasonably as he could. "Eventually it comes time for everybody to move on. So let me blaze the trail, and you boys pack up when you're ready. Just be sure to lock the door when you leave."

The Devil went to California. He rented a beachfront cottage on the central coast, sold his various penthouses and Tuscan villas, and settled into the reflective life as comfortably as an anemone in a tide pool. Every day he walked to the local grocery for fresh fruits and vegetables, took long strolls into the dry, amber hills, or rented one of the nouvelle vague classics he'd always meant to watch from Blockbuster. He disdained malls, televised sports, and corporate-owned franchise restaurants. He tore up his credit cards, stopped worrying about the bottom line, and never opened his mail.

In his heyday, the Devil had enjoyed the most exotic pleasures that could be devised by an infinite array of saucy, fun-loving girls named Delilah. But until he met Melanie, he had never known true love before.

"I guess it's because love takes time," the Devil

reflected on the first night they slept together on the beach. "And time has never been something I've had too much of. Bartering for souls, keeping the penitents in agony, stoking the infernos of unutterable suffering, and so forth. And then, as if that's not enough, having to deal with all the endless whining. Oh, *please*, Master, *please* take my soul, *please* grant me unlimited wealth and fame and eternal youth and sex with any gal in the office, I'll do *any*thing you ask, please, *please*. When a guy's in the damnation game, he never gets a moment's rest. If I'd met you five years ago, Mel? I don't think I'd have stopped working long enough to realize what a wonderful, giving person you really are. But I've got the time now, baby. Come here a sec. I've got lots of time for you now."

They moved in together. They had children—a girl and a boy. They shopped at the health food co-op, campaigned for animal rights, and installed an energy-efficient Aga in the kitchen. They even canceled the lease on the Devil's Volvo and transported themselves everywhere on matching ten-speed racing bikes. These turned out to be the most wonderful and relaxing days the Devil had ever known.

Then, one afternoon when the Devil was sorting recyclable materials into their appropriate plastic bins, he received a surprise visitor from the past.

"How they hanging, big boy? I imagined all sorts of comeuppances for a useless old fart like yourself, but never this. Wasting your once-awesome days digging through garbage. Cleaning windows and mowing the lawn."

When the Devil looked up, he saw Punky Wilkenfeld climbing out of a two-door Corvette. Clad in one of the Devil's old suits, he looked out of place amid so much expensive retailoring.

Some guys know how to hang clothes, the Devil decided. And some guys just don't.

"Why, Punky," the Devil said softly, not without affection, "it's you."

"It sure is, pal. But they don't call me Punky anymore."

"Oh, no?" The Devil absently licked a bit of stale egg from his forepaw.

"Nope. These days people call me *Mr.* Wilkenfeld. Or better yet, the Eternal Lord of Darkness and Pain."

"It's like this, Pop," Punky continued over Red Zinger tea in the breakfast room. "When you took off, you left a trillion hungry mouths to feed. Mouths with razor-sharp teeth. Mouths with multitudinously forked tongues. Frankly, I didn't know what to do, so I turned the whole kit and caboodle over to the free-market system and let it ride. We went on the Dow in March, and by summer we'd bought out our two closest rivals—Microsoft and ITT. I even hear Mr. Hotshot Heavenly Father's been doing some diversifying. Doesn't matter to me, either. Whoever spends it—it's all money."

"It's always good to see a former employee make good, Punky," the Devil said graciously. "I mean, excuse me. *Mr.* Wilkenfeld."

Punky finished his tea with a long, parched swallow. "*Ahh,*" he said, hammering the mug down with a short, rude bang. "I guess I just wanted you to know that I haven't forgotten you, Pop. In fact, I've bought this little strip of beach you call home, and once we've finished erecting the condos, we'll bring in the offshore oil rigs, docking facilities, maybe a yacht club or two. Basically, Pop, I'm turning your life into scrap metal. Nothing to do with business, either. I just personally hate your guts."

The Devil gradually grew aware of a dim beeping sound. With a sigh, Punky reached into his vest pocket and deactivated his cell phone with a brisk little flick.

"Probably my broker," Punky said. "He calls all the time."

The Devil distantly regarded his former chargés d'affaires, whose soft pink lips were beaded with perspiration and bad faith. Poor Punky, the Devil thought. Some guys never learn.

"And wanta know the best thing about this shoreline redevelopment project, Pop? There's absolutely nothing you can do about it. You take it to the courts—I own them. You take it to the Board of Supervisors—I own *them*. You organize eight million sit-down demonstrations and I pave the whole damn lot of you over with bulldozers. That's the real pleasure of dealing dirt to you born-again types, Pop. *You* gotta be *good*. But I don't."

The Devil watched Punky stand, brush himself off, and reach for his snakeskin briefcase. Then, as if seeking a balance to this hard, unaccommodating vision, he looked out his picture window at the hardware equipment littering his backyard. The Devil had been intending to install aluminum siding all week, and he hated to see unfulfilled projects rust away in the salty air.

"One second," the Devil said. "I'll be right back."

"Sorry, Pop, but this is one CEO who believes in full steam ahead, *toot toot*! Keep in touch, guy. Unless, that is, I get in touch with *you* first."

But before Punky reached the front door, the Devil had returned from the backyard with his shearing scissors. And Punky, who had belonged to the managerial classes for more aeons than he cared to remember, was slow to recognize any instrument used in the performance of manual labor.

"Hey, Pop, that's more like it," Punky said slowly, the wrong sun dawning from the wrong hills. "I could use a little grooming—if only to remind us both who's boss. Here, at the edge of this cloven hoof? What does that look like to you? A hangnail?"

Punky had crouched down so low that it resembled submission.

At which point the Devil chopped Punky Wilkenfeld into a million tiny bits.

"Seagulls don't mind what they eat," the Devil reflected later. He was standing at the end of a long wooden pier, watching white birds dive into the frothy red water. "Which is probably why they remind me so much of men."

The Devil wondered idly if his life had a moral. If it did, he decided, it was probably this:

Just because people change their lives for the better doesn't mean they're stupid.

Then, remembering it was his turn to do bouillabaisse, the Devil turned his back on the glorious sunset and went home.

Dazzle's Inferno

On a bleak November afternoon, while searching Highway 1 for an errant grandpup, Dazzle was snapped up by the SPCA and transported to the Animal Preservation Facility in Ventura, where he was printed, tagged, and impounded. "Preservation, hah, that's a laugh," Dazzle thought out loud as he was corraled into a mesh-wire compound. "Elimination of unreliable elements—*that's* more like it." By the time the shock wore off, Dazzle found himself immured by hypersanitary living conditions, cold-eyed animal welfare agents, and just about the sorriest collection of fellow mutts he had ever encountered.

"So I don't get it," Dazzle opined to anybody who would listen. "They deworm and delouse us, shoot us full of antibiotics, and when they think we're *healthy* enough, they throw us into this steel trap where we're expected to piss through the floors and drink out of rusty bowls. I mean, just look at this bedding, for Christ's sake. Is that a vinyl bean-bag chair or what? It's not comfort they're aiming for. It's something you can hose down, turn over, and reuse."

But rather than acknowledge his admittedly wrong-footed efforts at communication, Dazzle's fellow inmates either growled him away from their Nibbles or tried to mount him from behind and fuck him in the bottom.

"Hey, cool it!" Dazzle yelped, shaking free the latest serial perv with a hippy little snap. "You're barking up the wrong sycamore, bud. Nothing personal, either. It's just the way I happen to be."

Everywhere Dazzle turned, his cellmates were engaged in closet-busting activities, as if the very meaning of privacy had been turned inside out. They freely licked themselves and one another in every conceivable orifice; they poohed in the water bowl and dry-humped the bedding. And at the drop of a hat, they fought fiercely and endlessly over nothing, gouging and clawing and gnashing and shredding.

"If I told you once I told you a thousand times—stay away from *my* Nibbles!"

"Don't look at me that way or even *think* what you're thinking!"

"What's oozing from that pustule? Do you mind? Mmm, thanks. I needed that."

"I hate you I hate you I hate you I hate you."

"Hate me hate me hate me hate."

There were times when Dazzle felt like a bit of meat hurled into the gasketed vortices of some mighty machine—a process for producing pies, say, or a sharply pronged chicken defeatherer. Everything that was most

mindless about dogs had been amplified out of all pro-
portion until all you could hear was the raucous metal
whine of denaturized stuff: bile, testosterone, greed, fear,
denial, and rage.

"You guys are the end of language," Dazzle told them,
curled up with disbelief in a corner. "You guys are the end
of rational thought. At this point we should be banding
together, singing songs to bolster our spirits, and raging
against the darkness. It's supposed to be us against them;
but with you guys, it's everybody against each other, tooth
and claw. Believe me, you guys gotta think straight for a
minute and make a choice. Either work to a common
purpose, or die alone. It's up to you."

"Where are the puppies, Daddy?"

"They're in another pen, sweetheart. These are the
grown-up doggies. The ones that got lost from their masters and nobody wants."

"Can we see the puppies now?"

"It never hurts to look, sweetheart. Like this doggy
here? He looks nice, doesn't he?"

Of all the indignities Dazzle had suffered, visiting
hours took the biscuit. Every weekday afternoon,
human beings in search of pliable pets were hustled
past on their way to the nursery, but they never stayed
long. After all, Dazzle reflected, nobody wants a self-
formed dog with his own thoughts and opinions. They
only want malleable, just-weaned babies they can mold
into treatmongers and guarddogs. Dogs who take what
you give them and never complain.

"I don't know, Daddy," the little girl said. "Why's he
looking at me so funny?"

"What do you mean, sweetheart? He's a pretty dog and

well mannered. He's just looking at you that way because—oh, I see. That is a funny look, isn't it? It's almost as if, as if . . ."

"It's like he doesn't like me, Daddy. But I'm not important enough to make him mad."

Bingo, Dazzle thought, gazing into the moppet's muddy brown eyes. Dazzle had never been terribly fond of human beings, but at least adults remembered to feed, water, and run you on occasion. Moppets, however, were always dressing you in doll clothes and tempting you with fast-food sandwiches and candy bars, as if you were too stupid to know twenty-four-carat crap when you saw it.

"Yes, darling, well, at least we gave the older doggies a sporting chance. Now, let me at those puppies! I think we should get a cute one and teach it all sorts of neat tricks."

"And it'll love me, won't it, Daddy? It'll love me more than anything. Even more than its own mommy!"

As the human visitors were ushered happily toward the nursery, where the pulse-pleasing cacophony of puppies filled the air like Muzak, Dazzle sighed with relief.

"My mommy was a neurotic bitch who lived behind a Dumpster," Dazzle thought after them, with a sense of quiet grandeur that only comes to those without hope. "And just for the record, chickie—you'll never take the place of *my* mommy."

They were all riding the same short conveyor belt to nowhere.

"You're tagged with this number, right? Around your neck. There, right *there*," Dazzle explained to the only dog who paid attention, a mixed wire-hair spaniel named Grunt with weird rubbery growths on his face. "And this number corresponds to the day of the month you were first processed, see? And when the thirty days are up, so are you. Poof. In South America, you've entered the ranks of *los desaparecidos*. And once that happens, it's like you've never been born."

Grunt was an unusually curious dog, part border collie on his father's side, who could sit for hours watching words issue from Dazzle's lips like glistening soap bubbles.

"You talk and I'll listen," Grunt steadfastly assured Dazzle. "It's like I got this reverse attention deficit thing going, *comprende*? I gotta keep staring at somebody, or I kinda go totally nuts."

In many ways, Grunt was the perfect friend for a dog like Dazzle, who liked to talk but was never so wild about listening.

"Human civilization is like this big machine, right?" Dazzle would continue, inspired by Grunt's unwavering attention. "Turning everything we are into everything we're not. Surplus value, commodities, spin, psychobabble, culture, landfill, graphs. To creatures like that, we aren't dogs. We're just a record of human efficiency, a pie chart to be displayed at the next managerial review. How quickly we were eliminated—that'll matter. How cost-efficiently we were incinerated—that'll matter, too. But the moral and philosophical reasoning behind *why* we were needed in the first place, well, nobody will waste too much time on *that*. They aren't the sort of questions that can be submitted with your next budget proposal. If you want to build yourself a nice golden parachute, you'd better leave those questions alone."

"Absitively!" Grunt yipped. "Posolutely!" Grunt was so deeply affirmative that he seemed to glow with an inner authority. "Tell it like it is, Dazzle! I could listen to you all night!"

Sometimes Grunt was so exhaustingly attentive that Dazzle actually ran out of things to say. He looked at Grunt looking at him and eventually lay down on the cold mesh floor, closed his eyes, and felt Grunt's intensity drilling through the back of his neck.

"Are you going to sleep?" Grunt asked wonderingly. "Well, okay, you know where to find me. Sometimes I take these little naps with my eyes open, I don't even know it's happening. So don't be startled, Dazzle, if you wake up to find me already here."

On the same rainy afternoon that the ward's biggest bullies, Spike and Fatso, were led to the dispensary yipping "Snacks! Bitches! Sunlight! Snacks!," an especially bland, perspicacious visitor arrived at the Adult Male Holding Facility. Her name was Dr. Harriet Harmony, and she wielded a clipboard, a severely bitten plastic ball point, and a wallet-size electronic calculator.

"Uh oh," Dazzle told Grunt, who was chewing his toes in a way that Dazzle found particularly revolting. "I don't like the look of this babe what so ever."

Dr. Harriet Harmony had received her B.A. in animal husbandry from Princeton, and her doctorate from Iowa State. She wore sensible shoes; wire-rim bifocals; and a crude, hasty bob that might well have been self-administered with a prison shaving mirror and a cereal bowl.

"Vivisection," Grunt growled darkly and crawled under Dazzle's tail to hide. It was the longest word Dazzle had ever heard spoken by a dog to whom he wasn't intimately related.

"Which of you big boys would like to go with Dr. Harmony?" asked Maggie, the floor supervisor. To get their attention, she brushed her hand across the mesh with a metallic thip-thip-thip sound, as if she were petting a huge, scaly reptile. "Guess what Dr. Harmony has at *her* housy-wousy? A big bowl of meaty *Alpo*."

The very word struck a chill into Dazzle's heart. Whenever human beings were about to do something truly unconscionable to a dog, they always promised him Alpo.

Flipping through the forms on her clipboard, Dr. Harmony confirmed the identity of one random mutt after another with a brisk switch of her pen. Check. Check.

"Too big," she noted out loud. "Too furry. Too pure-bred. Too mean."

It's times like this you believe in precognition, Dazzle thought, for from the moment Dr. Harmony appeared, Dazzle knew they were meant for each other—whether he liked it or not.

"What about this one?" Dr. Harmony asked.

She wasn't looking at Dazzle. She was looking at Adult Male No. 4243.

"Oh, isn't he a cutey," Maggie enthused. She already had Dazzle's attention, but she wanted much more. "Would you like to take a little walk with Dr. Harmony, you big cutey-wooty? You big hairy cutey you!"

Dazzle was allowed no time at all to console poor Grunt, who leaped and spun fiercely about as if he were being teased by a bone on a bungee cord.

"Don't worry, Grunt!" Dazzle shouted as he was pulled down the corridor on Maggie's leather leash. "If they torture me to death for the sake of improving human deodorants, at least I'll glimpse the blue sky again on my way out! And come to think of it, who wouldn't like to see some improvement in human deodorants, anyway? I'm all for it. What about you?"

For once, Dazzle's words had a resounding effect on his fellow dogs.

"Human smells!" they barked. "How we hate those awful human smells!"

"Whatever you do, don't let them hook anything to your testicles!" Grunt shouted in dim, diminishing yips.

And Dazzle smiled over his shoulder, flattered by the concern.

"If they want to hook anything to my testicles, they'll have to call my old vet in Reseda Hills and find out where he buried 'em. Take care of yourself, pal. And keep a tight asshole. Dig?"

It happened so fast that Dazzle never knew what hit him. He was retagged and reregistered, driven to West Los Angeles in a minivan, and reconfined in a smaller, tidier private accommodation in the recently endowed, Egyptian-style monolith of the Center for Applied Sciences at UCLA.

"Welcome to your new home," Dr. Harmony told him and curtly disappeared with her clipboard.

The accommodation was equipped with a water dispenser, a yelp-activated shower, and, lo and behold, a fresh bowl of Alpo.

"You're not fooling me with that old trick," Dazzle grumbled, and curled up disdainfully on the floor beside the clean fragrant cotton futon, adorned with bright, squeaky rubber toys like a canine odalisque. "You guys tell me what you want, and I'll decide if I'm giving it to you or not."

Within the hour, Dr. Harmony returned with her senior research supervisor and a pretty young court reporter named Carol.

"Welcome to UCLA," Dr. Marvin said slowly, as if he

were addressing a roomful of multinational students in a TEFL course.

The stenographer, cued by Dr. Marvin's nonaggressive smile, began to type.

Tappety-tappety-tappety-tappety.

"We hope you have found everything satisfactory."

Tip-tippety-tappety-tap-tappety-tap.

"And that you will graciously accept this opportunity to meet with the recently endowed Department of Animal Linguistics on an equal footing."

Tappety-tappety-tappety-tappety-tip.

"Let's put the ugly days of blood-hurling demonstrators and bad publicity behind us. With the kind and generous support of Animals Alive!, the officially registered charity of sport-shoe entrepreneur and animal-lover R. Wallace MacShane, we are about to forge a new era in human-animal relations."

Tappety-tip-tappety-tap-tap-tap-tap. Tap.

The moment Carol stopped typing, Dr. Marvin and Dr. Harmony exchanged curt, professional smiles. Then, in one smoothly synchronized motion, they entered Dazzle's cell, crouched, and offered their hands in a gesture of olfactory openness and good faith.

Dazzle couldn't work up enough enmity to growl. Had he his druthers, he would have liked to forge a new era of human-animal relations in Dr. Harmony's fat butt.

At which point Dr. Harmony slipped one hand into the vest pocket of her white lab coat, grabbed Dazzle by the haunch, and injected him with the largest, nastiest hypodermic he had ever seen.

"Yowzah!" Dazzle expostulated, starting to his feet as the numbness spread to his haunches, his ribs, his face, his tongue.

"You goddamn, goddamn . . ." Dazzle said.

And collapsed unconscious to the floor.

As Dazzle eventually learned, Dr. Harmony was inspired as a young girl by the best-selling fictional reflections of a sage, beneficent ape who had many wise things to say about the meaning of life and the harmonic convergences of nature. This ape bore no grudge against the Homo saps who had enslaved him in a zoo, since he pitied their collective inability to love, or be loved, with total sincerity.

"I guess that sensitive, beautiful creature taught me everything I know about Nature," Dr. Harmony confessed, drifting beside Dazzle in the dreamily burbling laboratory. "And as a result of his patient instruction, I learned to look beyond my petty, callous concerns, and explore the spiritual oneness of Nature. I learned that this oneness invests every living creature on our planet, no matter how small, grubby, or ignoble. It invests doggies, and kitties, and monkeys, and me. I want you to know that I consider you a lot more important than some silly, tenure-achieving article in *Nature* or *Biology Today*, and I can only hope we won't remain divided from one another by the false dichotomy of humans-slash-animals. I'm hoping we'll learn to respect one another as friends."

Dazzle was not sure how long he had been drifting in the closed current of Dr. Harmony's voice. He only knew that she was with him, then she wasn't, and then she was again.

"I guess what I'm trying to say is that we make sacrifices every day for Nature. Mainly because in difficult, war-torn times like these, Mother Nature can use all the help she can get."

When Dazzle awoke he found himself drifting in a huge, gelatin-filled tank in a wide, omniscient laboratory buzzing with video cameras and metabolic gauges. His eyes were sewn open; his paws were bound in see-through plastic tape; and an array of multicolored, follicular implants sprouted from his forehead like a cybernetic toupé.

"We call it a syntactical eductor," Dr. Marvin explained, standing before Dazzle's immersion tank with the rapt, wide-open stare of a child observing his first jellyfish at the aquarium. "For as you may soon understand, it's not words that generate meaning, but how those words are *arranged*. Subject and object, subjunctive and possessive, predicate and noun. The invisible logic that our brains weave of things, thoughts, and sensations. Deprived of semantics, we drift through a universe of disparity and contradiction. We don't know which way is up, or how far, or how to get there from here. We can't distinguish us from them, or him from her, or being from what used to be. No wonder you poor animals have such a hard time, herded mindlessly from one form of oppression to another, trapped by your limited comprehension, which only processes one thought at a time, such as Sit, Shake, Dinnertime, and Kiss-kiss. But today, Mr. Adult Male No. 4243, is the first day of the rest of your life. In receiving the Promethean gift of syntax, you will engage everything that comes with it. Synchronicity, intention, history, and causation."

At this point, Dr. Harmony stepped forward, holding a compact digital microphone, as if she were about to perform a high-tech karaoke.

"**Me like doggy**," Dr. Harmony enunciated, placing her flat, bitten fingernails against the glass of Dazzle's container. "**Me protect doggy. Doggy help me. Me help doggy.**"

There was something so horrific about the concentrated sincerity of Dr. Harmony's face that Dazzle couldn't bear to watch. Meanwhile, the electronically translated words clanked hollowly among his wired synapses, like chords plunked out on a child's xylophone.

His brain literally rattled with words.

"**Me talk nice to doggy,**" Dr. Harmony continued, miming the removal of fragrant words from her mouth, and presenting them to Dazzle like red rubber chew toys.

"**Doggy speak nice to *me*? What do you say, doggy? Me want to hear your words *very much*.**"

The inflections pinged in Dazzle's brain like the chimes of a cash register. And for the first time that Dazzle could remember, a human question mark developed into an invitation to speak.

Dazzle wished he were the sort of dog who could resist that invitation. But, of course, he wasn't.

"Spuh," Dazzle said. His metal voice rasped on the overhead speakers like a dog chain sliding across a stainless steel bowl. "Spuh, spuh."

Until a miraculous, deep-timbred voice emerged into the wide laboratory like James Earl Jones announcing the divine presence of CNN:

"Spuh-spuh-spare me the condescending horseshit, sister. And you got a lot of nerve, talking to me like *I'm* stupid."

For seven days and seven nights, Dazzle raged at the blunt world, hitting it with all the stuff he had in him: iron negativity and rage. It was a bizarrely liberating experience.

He raged at their illusions about democracy: "Okay, so

every country's divided up between these two cosmetically antithetical political parties, and they both represent people with money. Isn't that what's called a tautology? Two absurdly redundant propositions. That's what your political process looks like to me, honey. A human fucking tautology."

He raged at their illusions about dogs: "Of *course* we roll over and wag our stupid tails and follow you around the house, mewling and twitching at every scrap of affection. We're prisoners, for christsake. If we live in the basement, who else will feed us? Certainly not that idiotic mailman, who shoves rolled-up newspapers through the grate. And what do rolled-up newspapers represent? Mind control, torture, irrational submission to authority. If you ask me (and I hate to remind you, but you *did* ask me, and now I'm telling you), that mailman deserves all the grief he can get."

And without mercy or remorse, he raged at their illusions about Nature: "So what do you tell yourself about this grand project, Dr. Harmony, alone in your bed at night? Personally, I've got you pegged as a *Dances with Wolves* girl—wow, you should have seen yourself flinch. You've probably got the director's cut on DVD, right? And you light all your scented candles after a hot bath in some slinky robe, and stretch out on that crummy student couch you've still got with the itchy osier fabric, and you *are* native woman, aren't you, Dr. Harmony? And you will purify your Kevin baby with that adorable mustache of his and that oh-so-striking uniform, waiting for him to carry you into your tepee where you will teach him the magic ways of—cool it, Dr. Harmony, okay, I'll stop. But before I do, let me tell you something about Mother Nature. She's got crabs, and lice, and about eight billion venereal infections, and every ingrown hair and toenail usually develops into this oozing, life-threatening abscess. I *am* Nature, and do I sound wise and benevolent to you? You don't have to answer that, Dr. Harmony. What you think about me is written all over your face."

And ultimately, Dazzle raged at himself: "So I developed this extended family in the woods, right, with about a thousand steppups and stepgrandpups running around, bickering and fighting all the time and copulating with anything that moves, and it feels, it feels all right. It feels like what you guys call really "grown up." And I drift off, Dr. Harmony, into my sentimental dreams of wholeness and true being, tinged with irony and all that, but isn't everything tinged with irony, whether we like it or not? I mean, there I am, trying to teach the pups about being true to themselves, and doing the best they can and so forth, and meanwhile, what's happening to the world? Are dogs receiving progressively better treatment at the hands of you and your fellow saps? Are social institutions growing more progressive and humane? Is even the notion of equality between species being knocked around by college eggheads like yourself, not because dogs and cats are that smart or anything, but look at the lay of the land, Dr. Harmony. We sure as hell aren't any *stupider* than *you* guys. And when I get my bottom tossed into that dandy little concentration camp called Animal Preservation, well, I can't help thinking I brought it on myself somehow, and watching my fellow dogs brutalize one another in every conceivable fashion, it starts to feel like dying, Dr. Harmony. I don't know how else to explain it. Like I'm saying good-bye to every illusion I ever had about myself or my fellow dogs. I never wanted to die, Dr. Harmony, but something happened to me in the past few weeks, and these days I don't much want to live, either. So now that I can say what's on my mind, it's like all I've *got* to say is, well, nothing. Nowhere. Nohow. I'm left to wonder what *you* think about all this. Me, this chattering dog in this huge fishbowl, talking your head off for seven days and seven nights. What do *you* think about what I'm saying, Dr. Harmony? Answer that question, and it'd be like discourse. The first step toward something bigger than us both. What do *you* think about *me*?"

Not so surprisingly, Dr. Harmony missed her cue. Flanked by Dr. Marvin (who was writing a grant proposal) and the court reporter (who was tappily transcribing the ineluctable data that was Dazzle), Dr. Harmony gazed into the translucent goo as if trying to remember where she left her car keys.

"What I think," Dr. Harmony said emptily. The pistons missed a beat, then another. "What I think. *You* want to know what *I* think."

Even Dr. Marvin put down his Bic. And the court reporter, sensing a rare opportunity, reached for her warm can of diet soda to take a long, habit-quenching swallow.

"What I think is, well, I guess it's this. I think it's time for you to shut the fuck up, you stupid, annoying mutt."

They deactivated the recording machines, the lights, and the overhead fans, and everybody (with the obvious exception of Dazzle) went home for a well-deserved rest. It was the first time in a week that Dazzle had the opportunity to hear himself think. "You can either talk or think," Dazzle often told his fosterpups and grandpups. "But you can't do both at the same time."

When Dazzle was a teething pup, he knew the meaning of words before he knew the words themselves.

"Yip," he might tell mom, shaking his nose at the blue sky. Yip: clouds. Yip: cars. Yip yip: last night I saw a blazing meteor. Yip yip *yip* yip: I love catching buzzy flies in my mouth. In many ways, the words themselves hadn't mattered; for whatever Dazzle said, Mom smiled and licked his face.

I was speaking my *me*, Dazzle thought. And that's all that mattered to Mom. The language we inhabited when we lay together.

Yip, Dazzle thought now, drifting in the slow tremble of gelatin like a chunk of pineapple in a blancmange. Yip.

Flickery, unbidden images appeared on the screen of his imagination: a ball, a stick, a bowl of Nibbles. Yip. A cardboard box. Yip. A meaty bone. We speak our minds and other creatures never quite understand, Dazzle thought. Which is, I'm afraid, what language is all about.

The following morning, Dazzle made his demands known to the first employee to reactivate the overhead lighting.

"Basically, tell Dr. Harmony I'll be issuing a list of demands at oh-nine-hundred hours, so I'd like our court reporter present. And Dr. Marvin, of course, is more than welcome to attend—though what constitutes his actual purpose around here, other than signing his name to the articles his grad students write, presently eludes me. Also, it might be time to fly R. Wallace MacShane down from Marin. He and I need to share some major face time. Oh, and one more thing. I'd like you guys to stop calling me Mr. Adult Male No. 4243. My name, if you haven't noticed, is Dazzle."

Robert Wallace MacShane was an all-right kind of guy. He flew an energy-efficient private jet. He wore nonblend earth tone slacks, shirts, and shoes. He provided his nonunion domestic employees with a near-union-scale wage, pension scheme, and medical plan. And he always referred to his underpaid nondomestic employees as brave pioneers of the burgeoning Third World superstate.

"So here we are," Robbie said, clapping his warm, well-manicured hands together. Robbie liked to begin every *tête-à-tête* as if he were getting down to a happy weekend of dad-and-son touch football. "Dr. Marvin. Dr. Harmony. Me and, well . . . *you*."

A blink was the closest Robbie ever came to a shrug.

"Our, uh, our esteemed canine colleague who, through the aid of modern technology, has crossed the great cultural divide to speak to us from the hallowed, er—"

Dazzle didn't have time for this.

"Yadda-da-yadda-da," Dazzle said, eliciting a confused squeal of feedback from the overhead speakers. "Are the tapes running? They are? Then, Carol, will you begin transcribing? We should begin."

As a pup, Dazzle had spent many lazy afternoons in front of the television watching black-and-white reruns of *Thin Man* movies on *Dialing for Dollars*. In these highly unrealistic, Depression-era mysteries, William Powell and Myrna Loy wandered from one dinner party to another, uncovering corpses, making friends with heartsick young people, and getting completely tanked along the way. Then, during the closing minutes, they would solve the accumulated crimes at a recitation attended by any and all surviving suspects, along with the local police chief, who couldn't catch a cold without their help. Meanwhile, their useless pooch, Asta, chewed the carpets and performed backflips like a trained bear at the circus.

This one's for you, Asta, Dazzle thought.

"So at first I figure it's just typical self-congratulation," Dazzle told them. "The victor's history lesson and all that. Big-time academics reaching down to shake the paw of lowly canines, airplay on all the networks, drive-time talk and late-night panel. Hey, before you know it, you've got your well-verbalized pooch appearing regularly on *Stupid Human Tricks*, or maybe he's one of the more lovable castaways on the next all-species edition of *Survivor*. They keep spelling your names right, and the name of this fine institution. This attracts more grants, and more notoriety, and pretty soon I'm like that sheep they cloned, that Daisy Whatever. It's not progress that matters—just the same public relations machine grinding out copy. At least dogs piss where they think it might do some good, but *you* guys. You just love the smell of yourselves, don't you? You just love to spread it around."

Robert Wallace MacShane firmly stood his ground and smiled the smile he was known for. It was the sort of smile he smiled very well indeed.

"I'm listening," he said. And for the first time that morning he took a chair beside Dr. Harmony, who was slurping Red Zinger from a hefty-sized *Dr. Dolittle II* promotional mug. "My conference call isn't till ten-thirty."

If Dazzle could have smiled, he would have given R. Wallace MacShane a run for his money. Instead, Dazzle leaned back in his roomy mind and produced the only emphasis at his disposal.

He *modulated*.

"Ahh," Dazzle's smoother, warmer voice said out loud. "I think we're almost done."

At which point Dazzle let them have it.

"But one way or another, things don't look good for

yours truly. I'm not exactly lovable or charming or telegenic. I don't do tricks on demand. And you've clearly dumped a good chunk of your endowment wiring me up to these doohickeys, with what to show for it? An irascible, antisocial canine who won't exactly be barking your praises to Rosie. Which leaves you with two choices. You can perform an expensive surgical reversal, unhook and delinguify me, then suture up all these exposed nerves and whatnot. Or you can cut all the cables and toss me in the Dumpster, right along with Adult Males Nos. 1 through 4242. I'm guessing you've targeted me for the Dumpster. What are the odds, guys? You wanta make me famous or make me dead?"

Dr. Marvin made a point of not looking at Dr. Harmony.

Dr. Harmony made a point of looking directly at Dr. Marvin.

Ha, Dazzle thought. I think we call that gin.

"Which leaves me swimming in this soup," Dazzle resumed smartly. "Wondering what I can offer you guys in exchange for my sorry bones back. And that's when I think the magic word."

Dazzle paused for effect.

"Nibbles," he said finally.

R. Wallace MacShane's smile suffered a noticeable glitch, as if his software had gone slightly ditzy.

"Nibbles," Dazzle continued. "They're the one common denominator, right? Nibbles at the Animal Preservation Center. Nibbles being pulverized by that whirring processor and pumping into my veins through these tubes. Nibbles, Inc., which is a minor subsidiary of Worldco Foods, which is itself coproprietor of Kidco Shoes, which is controlled by a panel of stockholders appointed by the very same CEO who appoints them, and who just happens to be sitting in this room. Robbie, our golden boy. Robert Wallace MacShane."

Robbie performed a curt little bow.

"It's like some basic elemental matter, the building blocks of the universe. Not atoms or energy or karma, but Nibbles, and it comes in a variety of flavors. Barbecued Ribs. Chicken Korma. Tuna Surprise. And for those diabetic dogs, there's sugar-free Veggie-Burger Plus, with all the flavor and protein of real meat. To hear you guys talking about Nibbles it's like you've discovered the Holy Grail or something, or the latest wonder dish whipped up by Wolfgang Puck. But the fact of the matter, as any dog can tell you, is that Nibbles taste like shit. Imagine dirt clods sprinkled with pesticides and chemicals, and you're in the same ballpark. You could soak this stuff in water for a thousand years and it would still taste like dirt clods. But what does it say on every Nibbles container ever produced in the history of this planet? It says; "Dogs *love* 'em!" Doesn't that make you wonder, Robbie? How you guys can produce Nibbles by the boatload and tell everybody dogs love 'em when nobody knows what dogs really love. Or, for that matter, even cares."

R. Wallace MacShane was getting his smile back, drumming neatly manicured fingers against his knee.

"My dog loves Nibbles," Robbie said smugly. "You should see Rex gobble them up."

It would make me sad, Dazzle thought, if it didn't make me so angry.

"What choice do you give Rex?" Dazzle asked. "I mean, does Rex *love* Nibbles more than, say, chicken-fried steak? Try putting a bowl of salsa-flavored Nibbles next to a hunk of chicken-fried steak, Robbie, and tell me which one Rex *really* loves better."

It all makes sense, Dazzle thought, watching the various faces watch him. Dr. Marvin: thinking about the grant appropriations committee that afternoon. Dr. Harmony: thinking about how much she loathes Dr. Marvin. And Carol, the stenographer, looking at her can of Diet Tab with a new, half-formed expression. Could she be thinking about possible connections between Nibbles and Diet Tab?

You could never be sure who would be the first person in a room to figure out what was really going on.

Robbie stopped drumming his fingers. Like any good negotiator, he knew this was the part where the guy holding all the cards offered you the only deal in town.

"Bring me the Yellow Pages," Dazzle instructed. "Turn them to Entertainment Lawyers and hook me to a phone line. Meanwhile, Dr. Harmony should get her skates on and hustle over to Animal Preservation, where my pal Grunt will be staring into the eye of a pretty nasty hypodermic right about now. Then, and only then, we'll talk contract."

After a few weeks of physio, Dazzle regained most of his old poise and swagger; and once the sutures began to heal, he booked himself and Grunt into the Ventura Doggy Motel, where they were treated to a hot flea shampoo; a chicken-fried steak; and a few sharp, well-received tonguefuls of strawberry schnapps. But even after Dazzle's hair had grown back over the scar tissue, his expression retained a weird, jigsawish incongruity, as if he were looking in two directions at once.

"Every so often, life takes us apart," Dazzle told Grunt on the day they were released back into the wide world. "And if we're lucky, we live long enough to put ourselves back together again. But along the way, we lose these little pieces of ourselves, and enduring these losses is what life is all about. Not paving ourselves over with cosmetic surgery, or spackle, or bad faith. But wearing our brokenness openly in our hearts and in our faces."

As per Dazzle's instructions, the Oldsmobile Town Car dropped them off at the intersection of PCH and Spring Valley Road. Unsurprisingly (at least to Dazzle), this intersection was marked by a self-illuminated Nibbles billboard, as big as a barn.

"Maybe I sold out, Grunt. I don't know. I've always believed in speaking the truth as well as my crude tongue allows, but sometimes you just want your life back. You just want to save your selfish sack of bones and go home."

Dazzle and Grunt were standing on the freeway's soft shoulder, gazing up at a rumpus-room-size bowl of multicolored Nibbles.

The billboard's caption read:

LATEST SCIENTIFIC ADVANCES CONFIRM

DOGS LOOOOOOVE NEW, IMPROVED

BOLOGNESE-FLAVORED NIBBLES MORE THAN FRESH MEAT!

Dazzle could abide the caption. What he couldn't abide was the tiny, asterisked confirmation which ran along the baseboard like the health warning on a cigarette pack:

*THESE STATEMENTS CONFIRMED BY EXPERIMENTS CONDUCTED AT UCLA ANIMAL RESEARCH LABORATORIES; DOCUMENTATION AVAILABLE ON REQUEST

Staring up at that monumental load of drivel, Dazzle couldn't help sighing at the enormity of language. It's we who should be speaking words, he thought. But more often than not, it's words that speak *us*.

Despite his brave face, Dazzle did not feel victorious, smug, or even clever. In fact, he didn't feel much of any-thing—only weakness in his heart, and the deep impress of too many years. Standing at the junction of four roads, he couldn't even decide which way to turn, or why one road might be better than any other.

They might have sat there all day had it not been for the surprising impatience of Grunt.

"Sometimes we have to fight like hell just to keep a little of what we already got," Grunt said. "Wind, trees, rocks, sunlight, clouds, you name it. Not just our own selfish skin—as you put it—but our genuinely selfless pleasure in everything that *isn't* us. The best we have to offer the world and everybody in it is who we *are*, Dazzle. And to my mind, that's justification enough to carry on."

It was the sort of wisdom Dazzle had always aspired to, perhaps when he was older and less prone to querying. Simple, regular, heartfelt, and as true as you could make it. And here it was, just when he least expected it, coming straight at him through the unremarkable voice of a fellow dog.

Who would've figured?

"Someday, Dazzle, you'll stop talking long enough to listen," Grunt said gently. "Hell, who knows? You might even learn a thing or two."

At which point Grunt showed Dazzle the quickest route out of town.

Heaven Sent

As a child, Daniel had envisioned heaven as a fragrant, sunny place filled with beatific angels, perpetually mild weather, and a lot of ambient music of the New Age variety. Eventually, however, he learned (and much sooner than he expected) that it was more like the desultory bar of some unfrequented bowling alley where morose, underfinanced people sat around all day drinking Manhattans and gin fizzes. They listened to scratchy Frank Sinatra records on the jukebox and rattled dice in leather-upholstered cups, which they periodically slammed down on the wooden countertop. The women were all overweight and slightly tarnished-looking; they wore excessively tight, synthetic-blend blouses and fake suede cowboy boots, and either their hair was discolored from too many recent dye jobs, or they wore cheap artificial wigs unraveling around the scalpline. The men wore faded polyester slacks, and bowling shirts emblazoned with promotional advertisements for candy bars and sports equipment. Everybody smoked generic filter cigarettes, ate roasted peanuts from a bowl, and watched scoreless ball games on the flickering black-and-white overhead TV.

As if placed there by Providence, an empty stool awaited Daniel at the poorly varnished oak bar.

Daniel took his seat and pondered his reflection in the gilded mirror behind the liquor racks. He was still wearing his frazzled beige sweatshirt and Levi's cords. He didn't look particularly bad for someone who had just died, but he didn't look particularly good, either.

"I guess I'll have a rum and Coke," Daniel said.

The bartender was skinny and dangerous-looking in his stained white apron and green flannel shirt.

"We're all out of Coke," the bartender said. "All we got is Diet Tab."

Daniel thought about this for a minute. He picked the plastic fragments of a recently opened cigarette package from the bar and deposited them in a dented aluminum ashtray.

"Make that a rum and Diet Tab then," Daniel said.

The drink contained carbonated chemicals, a dash of food coloring, and a dim impression of alcohol. It was accompanied by a free pack of generic menthol cigarettes.

"Part of this new promotion we're trying," the bartender said, gesturing at the room's collectively smoking inhabitants. "If it takes off, we may turn it into one of the divine heavenly services around here."

Daniel sipped his drink and replaced it on the counter.

"I don't smoke," Daniel said.

The bartender emptied the aluminum ashtray into a large green plastic bin.

"Maybe you should start," the bartender said.

"We had to do *some*thing," St. Peter explained that afternoon during the daily convocation ceremony. The wide auditorium was decorated with limp green and blue crepe paper streamers. St. Peter was standing on the raised podium, framed by an elephant-size sheet of butcher's paper that announced; WELCOME TO THE CLASS OF FEBRUARY 17, 2002! When St. Peter spoke, his voice was punctuated by shrill ellipses of feedback. "I mean, if you newcomers . . . could've just seen this place three, four centuries ago. We're talking about over . . . crowding of near-catastrophic proportions. We're talking about deteriorating public services, a withering economic . . . index, increased moral cynicism, and seriously bad vibes. The seraphs and cherubim were even talking about, I hate to say it, but . . . *unionization*. There were Communistical epithets being uttered downstairs in the . . . kitchen. Words like *proletariat*. Words like *mode of production*. Words like *class consciousness* and *surplus value*. This place was going to hell . . . in a handcar, ladies and gentlemen. And it came time to effect some serious reprioritizing around here!"

Daniel was sitting on the wooden bleachers with his fellow recruits, many of whom were browsing through smudged, badly mimeographed copies of the *Guide to Heavenly Services Instruction Booklet*.

"Now, if you'll all turn to page three in your booklets," St. Peter told them, "I'll begin by discussing the excellent peer-support counseling program we offer. And those of you who didn't receive a booklet, please try sharing with your neighbors. We seem to be a little short of supplies."

• • •

"Heaven isn't a place," Daniel's bunkmate, Nick Dougherty, explained after lights out. Daniel had been assigned to share Nick's small, beige dormitory cell, which contained two-tiered bunk beds, a lime-stained porcelain washbasin, and a tatty blue towel. "Heaven's a sense of history and destination. We plan for it; we learn to imagine it; and we gradually invest it with reality, every minute we're alive. You can't expect it to be this always-perfect place that's just waiting for you to arrive. It's more like a place you learn to expect. But with a percentage value subtracted to cover depreciation."

Daniel was lying on the top and watching his pale toes extrude from the itchy, military-style wool blanket. He was balancing a glass ashtray on his stomach and smoking a generic menthol cigarette.

"I just realized something," Daniel said. "This is where people go when they die, right? And death is what you might call a radically egalitarian concept. So why aren't there, like, any black or Latin people here? Or any Asians?"

"Like I told you, pal. We imagine the best that we're capable of imagining and then we get it, whether we like it or not. Take yourself, Danny boy. White, middle-class, a former assistant to the undersecretary of the vice president of a third-rate weapons manufacturer in Burbank. For you, heaven's sort of like Reseda or Coalinga. Relatively clean, relatively safe, relatively—on the surface—*nice*. But without the smog. Or the sun, either, for that matter."

The overhead electric bulb began to dim, and Daniel felt himself diminishing in the tiny room, smaller and smaller, like a cube of dry ice deliquescing on a plate. Daniel crushed out his cigarette.

"Actually," Daniel said, "I always sort of dreamed I'd spend eternity somewhere like Bermuda. Lots of sun, beautiful girls, free food, and happy hour all day long."

Daniel heard Nick utter a long, exasperated sigh. Then, without warning, Nick punched the underside of Daniel's mattress with a terrific right cross. The rusty springs chattered.

"You just don't get it, do you, Danny boy? Heaven isn't the everlasting fulfillment of what you *dream*. Heaven is the everlasting fulfillment of what you think you *deserve*."

Daniel was assigned to Heavenly Sales and Promotion, where, every morning after breakfast, he tried to generate advertising copy in a small, semiprivate cubicle cluttered with cardboard file boxes. Then, before he went home each evening, he attended the daily business conference and listened to his group actualization coordinator issue the day's official marching orders.

"This isn't your usual two-bit operation," Duane Rogers told them, leaning over the long black conference table. Duane wore a fashionable wool-blend suit and a silk monogrammed tie. Like an outdoor café, he exuded a winsome aroma of eau de cologne and Perrier. "This is the goddamn Celestial City, for crying out loud. This is Golgotha, Pyramid Heights, the Castle in the Clouds. I give you guys a shot at the biggest operation going, the ultimate link in the great chain of being, and what thanks do I get? What kind of work do you guys expect me to read?"

Duane clutched the day's pile of interoffice memos in his immaculately manicured hand as if he were about to paper-train a small, shameful puppy.

"*This* is the thanks I get," he answered himself. "*This*

is the level of work I receive from the biggest bunch of unimaginative dildos in the entire heavenly galaxy!"

Duane shook open the stack of papers and realigned his sparkling cuff links. "Smoke generic menthol," Duane read scornfully from the top memo, "I like them a lot."

Duane passed his contempt slowly around the table, like a shrunken head on a stick. He continued, "Smoke generic menthol—they taste better than the others. Smoke generic menthol—me and my friends enjoy them often. Smoke generic menthol—what else you gonna do? Smoke generic menthol . . ."

Duane suddenly tore the entire stack of papers in half and shook them in the air like an angry pom-pom. "If you ever turn in copy like this ever again, I will personally nail your hands to the boardroom wall! I will eat your eyeballs! Now get *out* of my face! I can't stand to look at your ugly mugs another minute!"

"I think I'm getting my ulcer back," Daniel told Nick at home that evening. "Maybe I'll stay in tonight. You can go to the nightly sports event without me."

Nick was sitting on the floor cleaning his dismantled Smith & Wesson .227 automatic with one of Daniel's shredded I ♥ DIVINE PROVIDENCE T-shirts and some 3 IN 1 (oil).

"Sorry about your T-shirt," Nick said.

Daniel shrugged and sat down on Nick's bunk. Tonight was basketball night, which meant that he and the rest of the angelic choir would have to sit on hard wooden bleachers watching tall men shoot hoops. Then, in a prolonged, anticlimactic ceremony, the tall men would take turns reciting into a whistly microphone: "If it weren't for the love of God through Jesus Christ, I would never have learned how to play such excellent basketball."

"Where'd you get that?" Daniel asked.

Nick reattached the barrel with a pair of swift, meaningful clicks.

"I never go anywhere without serious firepower," Nick said.

They waited for lights out and made a break for the Far Precincts. The halls were musty, with leaning gray shadows everywhere. Every mile or so, they ducked into a convenient closet or alcove to avoid the distant echo of footsteps. The closets contained cardboard boxes stuffed with books and papers, gawky aluminum stepladders, empty paint cans, and stray vacuum attachments.

Nick withdrew his Smith & Wesson and deactivated the safety lever.

The distant footsteps paused, then slowly diminished.

After a few moments Nick said, "Let's go."

They passed through the Illumination Night. They passed through the New Jerusalem. They passed through the Heavenly City, the Heavenly Suburbs, and the Golden Arches. They passed through the Region of Bad Karma and the Slough of Despond. They passed through the Temptations of Ecclesiastical Polity. They passed through dark playgrounds, bankrupt shopping malls, and economically disadvantaged neighborhoods. Crushed glass was everywhere, and vulgar graffiti had been spray-painted across the blistering walls:

**FUMAR CIGARILLOS MENTOLADOS
ESTOS MUCHOS BUENOS**

The farther west they journeyed, the fewer emblems of heavenly authority they encountered. Eventually they reached Checkpoint Charlie, where a small bald man sat slumbering in a glass-paneled booth. The border was demarcated by a striped red and white toll gate.

"This is it," Nick said, poised with his pistol like a renegade detective on TV. "Time to separate the men from the boys."

Getting down on all fours, they crawled under the toll gate, stood on the other side, and brushed themselves off.

The man in the toll booth stopped snoring, sat up, and rubbed his eyes.

"Hey," he said. "Where do you guys think you're going?"

Nick replaced the pistol in his belt and nodded toward the dark stairwell.

"Where do you *think* we're going?" Nick asked.

The Nether Regions were filled with high blue skies and deep blue water. Waves hissed against the sandy beaches, and warm, fragrant winds ruffled the shaggy palms. In the shade of thatched huts and lean-tos, inhabitants dozed peacefully. Eventually Nick and Daniel came across a volleyball game, and Daniel recognized several friends from his old job back on Earth.

"Hey there, Danny boy!" they shouted. "It's been aeons!"

"It sure has," Daniel replied. They all shook hands and patted one another on the back. The well-developed men wore loud Bermuda shorts, and the well-developed women wore string bikinis. In fact, the entire group looked just as handsome, smug, and self-satisfied as they had back when Daniel worked with them at the Allied Defense Contractors plant in Burbank.

"What the hell you doing down here, Danny boy?"

they said. "We heard you went to Heaven with all the other Goody Two-Shoes."

Daniel shrugged at the blue horizon, visoring his eyes with his hand to cut the glare. "I always expected it to be a lot hotter here, you know?"

"Yeah," Daniel's old friends agreed, "so did we."

One fellow employee whom Daniel had especially disliked was Burt Friederich, who still wore the same handlebar mustache and mean, squinty look.

"You never did get the picture, did you, Danny boy?" Burt said, placing his unwelcome arm across Daniel's shoulder. "Sure, we doctored a few books in our time. Sure, we lobbied a few congressmen. And sure, maybe a few of the guns and boats we produced didn't quite work as advertised. But the important thing, Danny boy, is that we *believed* in a better life. Face it, Daniel: being good is for suckers. And in our scheme of things, we got what we *deserved* !"

Already Daniel's friends were drifting back to their volleyball game. The ice chests were filled with bottled ambrosia and fresh fruit. A portable radio was playing the best of Simon and Garfunkel.

Absolutely right, Daniel realized. The free market and the level playing field. Darwinian combat in the boardrooms, the exploitation of domestic and foreign labor, the relentless accumulation of wealth, the righteous contempt for human rights and public services. Daniel recalled a T-shirt Burt used to wear to all the company picnics:

**THE ONE WHO DIES
AFTER ACCUMULATING
THE MOST TOYS WINS**

Maybe it wasn't too late, Daniel decided. Maybe Daniel could believe in a better life, too.

"Psst," Daniel said just as Burt was turning away. "Hey, Burt!"

Burt turned. Daniel reached into his shirt pocket and removed a small, glimmering plastic package.

"Hey, guys!" Burt exclaimed merrily. "Danny boy brought smokes!"

Generic menthol turned out to be the most popular commercial product to hit the Nether Regions since frozen pizza.

And Daniel knew where he could always get more.

The Anti-Santa

The last house on the block was always the toughest.

"Ho ho ho, Jennifer Williams of seven seventy-five West Palmdale Avenue! *Mer*ry Christmas! *Mer*ry Christmas!"

"Are you Mommy's new boyfriend?"

"Absolutely not, little girl! Don't you recognize me and my solar-powered sleigh in the driveway there? How many hints do you need?"

"Santa Claus doesn't wear Levi's and a flannel shirt."

"That's because I'm not your normal, run-of-the-mill, commercially approved Santa. I'm the anti-Santa, Jennifer. But that doesn't make me anti-Christmas, oh, no. Not by a long shot."

"And his beard isn't blond and trimmed like that, and he doesn't wear cologne. You look more like that cute mountain man in *Dr. Quinn, Medicine Woman.*"

"Why, thanks. I don't actually trim it, but look, we're both in a hurry. Let's dig into our sack of wholesome treats and see what we have for Jennifer Williams this Christmas Eve. Why, it looks like you've been a *very* good girl. Anti-Santa has brought you *two* presents!"

"Let me see! Let me see!"

"As you can tell, Anti-Santa and his elves don't actually wrap their gifts up in gaudy, meretricious paper and bows, since that would only reinforce the fictive nature of high-consumer corporate propaganda."

"It's a big jar of pills."

"Not just any pills, Jennifer. What you hold in your hand is five hundred capsules of one-thousand-milligram timed-release Ester-C, the Cadillac of vitamin supplements. You take one of these suckers every morning with your orange juice and you'll enjoy the new year free from sniffles, flus, and long-term viral immunodeficiency."

"This present sucks, Anti-Santa."

"I'm sure you don't mean that, Jennifer. Anyway, here's another goody for you—a parsley plant to grow on the windowsill. Parsley cleanses the bad carbohydrates from your blood; if you take good care of it, this gift will take good care of you."

"I wanted a Barbie play set and a cell phone."

"No you didn't, Jennifer. Not really. That's what commercial culture *told* you you wanted. What you *really* want, what the long-term health and integrity of both your body and mind *require*—"

"These are the two worst Christmas presents I ever received in my life."

"Now honestly, Jennifer, that isn't very polite."

"You're knocking on *my* door, Anti-Santa. So you'll take what I give you."

"Well maybe, little Jennifer, but try to remember that I'm only—"

"Please leave, Anti-Santa, before I call the cops. Oh, and another thing."

Anti-Santa paused hopefully on the steps before he slung the huge, bulky bag over his shoulder. It was absurd, he thought, how we always hold out this vain, breathless expectation that a bad moment will get better. Even a moment as irredeemable as this one.

"Don't come back next year, Anti-Santa. Scratch me and Mommy off your list permanent, okay?"

<I'm sure she didn't mean it, sir> the glowing red eye on the dashboard solemnly intoned. **<You know how children get at this time of year.>**

The voice was designed to provide the same soft, seductive reassurance as HAL, in Stanley Kubrick's *2001: A Space Odyssey*. But since it communicated directly with the Radar Deployment Off-Base Simulator back in Tampa, everybody referred to it (naturally enough) as Rudolph.

"I guess so, Rudolph," Anti-Santa muttered slowly, unconvinced. "But I can't help feeling, maybe for just a few brief moments every so often, that kids don't really like me. They don't seem excited to see me at all."

<All that sugar and heightened expectation. It's a very powerful drug, sir. The children aren't always in their right mind. They need someone to bring them back down to earth.>

Anti-Santa gazed out at the sparkling night and wondered if he was the only person in the universe to appreciate what it was all about. Simplicity, vastness, cosmogony, and light. Not a lot of Third World–manufactured plastic crap adorned with tinsel and shiny foil.

"She said they were the worst presents she ever received in her life."

<She *is* only six years old, sir.>

"She seemed to think I was good-looking, anyway."

<That's something to build on.>

"And maybe we could, you know—we'd have to discuss it with the elves—but put a few more actual toys in the gift sack next year."

<Those wooden dreidels, handcarved by the native tribes of the Brazilian rain forest, seem to be quite a hit with the youngsters.>

"Yes, they don't actually throw them in my face or anything. Not like last year."

<And the comic books. All children like comic books.>

"Remind me when we get back to order more copies of *Mandela for Beginners*."

<You see, sir, that's what I admire about you. Even in adversity, you're preparing to take the next step forward. And well, uh-oh.>

The red light evinced a sudden blink, like a desktop computer catching up with its own streaming data.

<Course correction requested, sir. Perhaps it might be best to adjust our longitudinal axis a half degree eastward before—>

Anti-Santa felt it rise from the nub of his colon. It wasn't his soyburger from supper or even the fruit smoothie. It was something both more intangible and more distinct.

"It's him, isn't it?"

<I see no reason, Sir, especially when you're just starting to feel better—>

"We won't be changing our course for anybody tonight, Rudolph. Especially not for *him*."

It was as if speaking his presence made it real, and before Anti-Santa could anchor himself to his ergonomically designed seat, a meteor blaze and sonic clap struck the sky with tangle-horned reindeer and snow-dusted hooves and plump piles of velour-sacked prezzies as fairy dust sprayed across the surface of starlight tinkling with a memory of bells. Anti-Santa could learn to live with the reindeer and the prezzies—but the fairy dust, throbbing with false cheer and subliminal advertising. The fairy dust was truly unbearable.

"Ho ho ho! Merry Christmas!" cried the Old Man through his fat, plummy face, heated into veiny splotches by several generations of imbibing cheap Tokay. *"You pretentious, silly little do-gooder! Merry Christmas! Merry Christmas to all and to all a good niiiii—"*

And then he was gone again in the flash of his own anticipation, like light chasing itself into a black hole. The sky resounded ominously.

<Sorry, sir. I tried to warn you.>

Anti-Santa felt the fragile truthfulness of night relapse around him, wavering like a mirage. It felt so thin and impalpable now. It made him want to cry.

Seeing the Old Man again was hard. But seeing him leave was always harder.

"That's okay, Rudolph. We can take anything he throws at us. Now let's get to work and land this boat. It's time to deliver those Amnesty International lifetime memberships to the kids in St. Pete."

By 4:00 AM, it was nearly impossible for Anti-Santa to maintain his spontaneous goodwill for humanity. Cynical, enervated, and footsore, he began speaking his yuletide greetings woodenly, as if reading them from a three-by-five file card.

"Ho ho ho, everybody. Merry Christmas and so forth."

"Hold it right there, pal. Where you think you're going with that burlap sack?"

"Oh, hi, Eugene, it's me. Anti-Santa. I just have these sugar-free candied apples to deliver to the residents of your cozy little gated community, along with the latest paperback edition of Noam Chomsky's *Deterring Democracy*. Could you please be careful where you point that thing, Eugene? You realize that America suffers nearly twenty thousand needless gun-related fatalities each year, most of which are the result of accident or misuse."

"How'd you know my name? And where'd you get that weird-looking UFO-like dinghy?"

"You're Eugene Waterbury of six-oh-seven—"

"Hey, cut that out!"

"Your sons, Tony and Derek, are receiving Ammo Attack from, you know, the Old Man this year. Which is why you'll notice a couple of nonconfrontational-type playthings from yours truly under the collapsible tree. One's a board game I invented called Anti-Risk, which *isn't* about conquering the world or blowing up cities, thank God. Rather, the object is to negotiate peace settlements with your fellow players until you've achieved a world of total parity and mutual cooperation—"

"I'm calling the cops, Anti-Santa. Even if it is Christmas."

"I guess I should warn you, Eugene. I wouldn't do anything to hurt you, but I possess a green belt in aikido, and my sleigh is equipped with a protective force field that will deflect any—"

Bang.

"Shit, Eugene. I think you shot me."

"Damn right, Anti-Santa. Now, fly your contraption

off my turf or so help me. Sure as my name's Eugene Waterbury, you'll be digging a bullet out of both thighs."

Anti-Santa lost consciousness somewhere over the forty-second parallel.

"I thought Santa wore a red suit and said things like Ho ho ho."

"Help me get him on the gurney."

"This guy don't look like Santa to me. He looks more like that guy, that mountain man, right? On *Dr. Quinn, Medicine Woman*."

"He's not Santa, you idiot. He's the Anti-Santa. I saw a profile of him once on *Sixty Minutes Two*."

"When I was a kid I couldn't wait to visit Santa and his elves when they came through Macy's. Then I got older, right, and I just wanted to see Santa's elves. Hey, he's trying to say something."

"It's the thought that counts. It's the thought that counts. It's the thought that counts."

"Let's get some blood into him and see how he looks in the morning."

"It don't seem right, somehow. Santa Claus sleeping in the hall on a rusty gurney."

"He's not Santa, you idiot. He's—"

"I know, I got you. He's the Anti-Santa, which sounds kind of ominous, don't it? Like the Anti-Christ, triple sixes, and all that. Gregory Peck's wife getting shoved off the roof. I couldn't sleep for weeks after that flick."

"The Anti-Santa believes in telling it like it is. He hasn't got a publicist, and it's hurt him mediawise."

"Maybe. Or maybe it's those crappy presents he keeps giving."

"Here we go, pal. Maybe this'll help you sleep."

"This one elf, Chlöe, she had legs up to here, and wore this pea-green wraparound slit skirt. That girl got me through puberty, boy. And Santa—not *this* guy—but the *real* Santa I'm talking. He'd pretend he was listening to you tell what you wanted for Christmas? But the whole time he had his big knobby hand on Chlöe's ass. I couldn't blame him, neither. That old boy, one look at his ruby-red face and you knew. That was one Santa who knew how to have a good time."

They weren't dreams, exactly; they were more like periodic interventions of the real. Men and women moaning softly; crisp white shoes clacking on waxy linoleum; babies crying; the blossoming scents of disinfectant and blood. He didn't know where he was, and he didn't want to be anywhere else. It felt like one of those circular fades in a Looney Tunes cartoon.

"It's the worst time of year to feel unloved or underappreciated," Anti-Santa whispered softly. In his medicated fog, he saw his former lover, Chlöe, sitting across from him at the sawdust-strewn gingerbread table where they had once worked peacefully together under the beneficent (or so it had seemed) gaze of the Old Man. "You want to make the world a better place, and pass on some of the wisdom you've gleaned. You see these little kids, these bright little faces, and you want to make that brightness last, see yourself reflected in it somehow, you want to live forever. You don't want to dazzle them with fairy dust. You don't want to watch them grow inflated with consumer dullardry, chewing away obediently at huge, genetically modified steaks on a slab. You want them to grow and learn and maintain their, I don't know—their natural joy for life, their spontaneous, I guess you'd call it pleasure. Their ability to be pleased. Their ability to reply to the simple smells and tastes and textures of the world. Eventually you know it can't last. They'll be reprogrammed by TV and X-Box and the Home Shopping Network, and they won't take pleasure in anything anymore. They'll stop *replying*. They'll just start *responding*. They'll want to possess more plastic doodads than anybody else. They'll want to be better, happier, and wealthier than all their friends at school."

For the first few decades of their personal-slash-business relationship, Chlöe had listened to him with obvious concern, her eyes moist, her lips slightly parted. But eventually, as further decades passed, her expression grew cold and unresponsive. She began seeing other elves. She stopped returning his calls.

"I guess it might have helped if the Old Man had just, you know, listened to what I was trying to say," Anti-Santa told the last woman who had ever loved him. "If he hadn't just shrugged me off and snarled at all my ideas. And when I decided to start my own operation, he could have been more gracious about it. Maybe wished me luck, or told me to break a leg, I don't know, just something. Instead of calling me Mr. Know-It-All, Mr. Holier-Than-Thou, after everything he'd done and so forth. And then, I'm sorry, Chlöe. I'm sorry to get so emotional. But then never to write or call or ask how I was doing. To just dismiss my whole existence like that, and never, *never* understand that I was doing my best. That I loved the kids, too, and I just wanted, maybe once, to make one child happy. One child happy, Chlöe. That one child who wanted something most kids never find under their tree on Christmas Day."

• • •

In the lull before dawn, a stranger entered the ER and made his way to Anti-Santa's gurney. He was shrouded in fairy dust. The air tinkled synesthetically as he passed.

"Ho ho ho," he whispered. "Merry Christmas." The fairy dust darkled obligingly.

Gunshot victims and overdosed self-abusers and auto accidentees all stopped crying at once. All except for Anti-Santa, who felt wide, vertiginous spaces open around him, and the renascence of panic in his addled blood.

It couldn't happen like this. Not after all he had been through.

"Please not the fairy dust," he moaned dopily. "Anything but that."

"Ho ho ho." The Old Man's words whirled in the stale air like dust. "Merry Christmas, Mr. Know-It-All. Merry Christmas, Mr. Righteous Do-Gooder. Now let's see who's *really* been a good boy this year."

It was just past dawn when Anti-Santa awoke on a broken street in a broken city somewhere in midwestern America. The dashboard lights of his solar-powered sleigh thrummed solidly as they charged. He sat up. He felt his wounded thigh.

It was still bandaged. It still hurt.

"Oh, my gosh," Anti-Santa said with a sigh. "For a moment there I thought—I mean, I must have had the awfullest dream."

<The servomechanisms are almost functional again, sir> Rudolph modulated. **<When you're ready, I can prepare a mug of soy-enriched eggnog. And maybe another seaweed poultice for your leg.>**

It was one of those streets that made even Anti-Santa hesitate. Broken hypodermics and twisted condoms lay about the icy, smog-stained sludge like weird leaves. Houses and telephone poles were scarred with graffiti, gunshot, and police memoranda. And amid the jumble of all this unwelcome tinny information, it took a while to see anything that was simple, meaningful, and discrete.

She was standing directly in front of the sleigh. She was staring directly at him.

"I can't believe you came to see me, Anti-Santa. I can't believe you came to see me on Christmas morning."

She was precisely seven years, three months, and twelve days old. Fiona Washington's name had been on all his lists for years now, but this was the first time he had met her face to face.

<Ahem> Rudolph said. And gave Anti-Santa a nudge with the vibratory backrest.

It took Anti-Santa a second to catch up.

"Ho ho ho," Anti-Santa said distantly. "Merry Christmas. *Mer*ry Christmas, Fiona."

"It's so exciting, Anti-Santa. I mean, I've seen you on *Sixty Minutes Two* and I'm like your biggest fan. And here it is, the best part of Christmas already, before the latest stupid newspaper has been delivered, and you're here to see me, *me*, Fiona Washington. I can't tell you how happy it makes me, Anti-Santa. We've got so much in common it's ridiculous."

Anti-Santa tugged on the lapels of his down parka, feeling naked, off-kilter, and abashed. He was secretly ashamed about how much he needed to meet someone exactly like Fiona.

<Sir, we have a problem.>

"I'd go get Mommy, but she's crashed out on the sofa. Ever since Daddy got arrested she doesn't do anything all day long but watch TV and eat Pringles—"

"What's that, Rudolph?"

\<When you were at the hospital I delivered the last of the presents. I don't think we have anything left except maybe this.\>

Rudolph's mechanical arm extruded itself from the dashboard, bearing the remnants of Anti-Santa's bagged supper. The dolphin-friendly tuna from his long-digested sandwich had stained the brown paper with a macabre silhouette of Mickey Mouse.

It didn't seem possible. But suddenly all the wind went out of Fiona's sails.

"Oh, that's okay, Anti-Santa, that's okay, I guess. I mean, I shouldn't, I didn't expect anything really, I mean. I guess the real present is you came to see me, right? You came to see me, Fiona Washington, and nobody else."

Anti-Santa opened the bag and looked inside. There was only this last little object left in his entire sleigh, the only gift left to give. It wasn't much, but it looked a lot more intact and self-sufficient than Anti-Santa felt right now. He needed some sleep. He needed to wake again, like Fiona, to a brand-new world.

"It's not much, Fiona," Anti-Santa told her, his voice husky with emotion. "But it's all I've got."

Her bright eyes opened just a fractional bit wider.

"An egg, Anti-Santa? A hard-boiled egg?"

Anti-Santa smiled and shrugged. Sometimes life could be sad and happy at exactly the same time.

"It's like the ultimate container, isn't it, Anti-Santa? I could sit this on my bookshelf for years and it wouldn't rot, or break, or go bad. I mean, I heard these stories about the Chinese and they'd like save these eggs for hundreds of years before eating them. But I'm never going to eat *my* hard-boiled egg, Anti-Santa. Because you gave it to me. And every time I look at it, I'm going to remember you, and all the good things you've tried to do for children all over the world."

Anti-Santa was speechless. Then, just before the lapse of words grew too heavy to bear, he found heart enough to use a few old words one more time.

"Ho ho ho," he told her softly. "*Mer*ry Christmas."

And rode his sleigh, half asleep and smiling gently, all the way home to Tampa.

Pig Paradise

If it's true, as some German fellow has said, that without phosphorus there is no thought, it is still more true that there is no kindness of heart without a certain amount of imagination.
—Joseph Conrad, "Amy Foster"

Hubert was breaking into a sweat around his twitchy pink snout and trying to look casual with an icy glass of Évian. His bare bottom and the Naugahyde chair were starting to feel like a potentially embarrassing match.

"Look at me, Hubert. Why won't you *look* at me?"

Harry leaned across the Swedish modern office desk. His paws came together in a blunt arrow aimed directly at Hubert.

"I *am* looking at you, Harry. I mean, I'm looking at you right now."

Harry's red, lupine gaze was cool and unremitting.

"No, you're not, Hubert. You're looking at my paws. You're looking at my sharp teeth. You never look me in the eye, Hubert. Do you think I don't notice?"

Hubert rested the water glass against his monogrammed

red cotton weskit. He knew he should meet Harry's gaze, but he couldn't do it. He simply couldn't.

"I'm doing my best," Hubert told the glass. "I just wish, you know. I wish you wouldn't take it so personal."

"Take it personal," Harry said simply. "I shouldn't take it personal."

Hubert shifted in his squeaky seat. The hairs on the back of his neck bristled.

"You've got every right to be, well, not pissed off, Harry. I haven't done anything wrong. But your feelings, I'm sure your feelings *are* hurt, and I'm trying, Harry. I'm trying to understand."

Harry showed Hubert one digit after another of his right forepaw, ticking off each remonstrance. "You don't look at me. If you see me on the bus, you pretend not to. If you see me coming down the corridor, you duck the other way. If I ask for a meeting, you're too busy, you're ill, whatever. Everybody notices, Hubie. And how do you think it makes me feel? To be treated like some sort of, Jesus, some wild animal. Like I'm going to hunt you down and rip out your belly. Is that what you see when you look at me, Hubert? A savage beast that wants you for breakfast?"

Hubert looked out the window at the revolving corporate icon: a house-size aluminum kettle being stirred by a smiling wolf and an equally smiling pig.

Mama O'Brian's All-Veggie Pies
—today's food for today's world—

It was the first surge of pure anger that Hubert had felt in weeks.

"I didn't make me who I am, Harry. And I don't know what good you think you're doing putting so much pressure on me all the time. Like I can't come to work any-more without these guilt trips you're always laying on me about the way I feel, Harry, and I can't *help* the way I feel, but my whole inner being, Harry. According to you and the way you look at me, there's something wrong with how I feel deep inside."

Hubert thumped his red weskit twice with his hard, pale trotter. It gave him courage and a sense of resonance. He looked up.

Here's my eye contact, his expression told Harry. If this is what you want—you got it.

"Don't get upset," Harry said softly. "All I'm trying to say—"

"You're trying to say that I hurt your feelings, I'm not open-minded enough, I don't treat you like, like an equal or something. Like everybody's an equal and I'm sup-posed to walk down these corridors going Hi, hello, how you doing, equal equal equal, bing bing bing. But life isn't like that, Harry. Everybody's different, and everybody treats each other different, and I don't care what they say in the 'Employee Guidelines.' "

The tension seemed to bend in Harry's direction. Harry leaned back in his swivel chair, breaking into a sweat around his snout and collar.

"There's no need to raise your voice, Hubert. And as far as putting pressure on you, I never meant . . . this wasn't supposed . . ."

Hubert regained his breath. Now it was Harry who better keep out of *his* way.

"If you've got problems with my sales figures, Harry, then send me a memo and hey, better yet, copy it to the entire Sales Department and that's corporate, Harry. That's a matter we should set straight. But if you've got *personal* problems with me? Maybe you don't think I'm friendly enough, or respect you enough, or I don't look you in the eye, or whatever. You learn to *live* with that, Harry. Because I won't be harassed, Harry. I won't be harassed by *you* ever again."

"How'd it go, Mr. Armstrong?"

"I'd rather not talk about it, Stacey. Did my wife call?"

"She did. She and Mrs. Conroy left the kids with a sitter to attend some PTA thingie. She suggested you pick up dinner on the way home."

"How about those orders from the Franciscan winery?"

"On your desk."

"And the corporate earnings?"

"Ditto, Mr. Armstrong."

"Thanks, Stacey. For the next hour or so I don't want to be disturbed."

Stacey nodded curtly and turned back to her flat screen. Hubert watched her for a few seconds—just to make sure she wasn't watching him.

"Oh, and Stacey?"

"Uh-huh." The glowing spreadsheets were reflected by her pink eyes like a scheme of inner mathematics.

"I'll tell you if I need anything. Okay?"

"Okay, Hubie."

As Hubert shoved the door shut behind himself, it felt like letting all the air out of a balloon. He exhaled with a long, expiring whoosh and loosened his damp collar. He hyperventilated ten times and then held it, feeling the subsidence of blood in his brain. The room had gone white around the edges. The intercom on his desk began to buzz.

"Hubert Armstrong."

"How'd it go, old buddy? You marched past in the hall and didn't even look at me."

"Stan, I swear. I can't breathe or something. I still can't believe it. The things I said."

The intercom issued a long, staticky sigh.

"What sort of things, Hubert? What sort of things did you say?"

Hubert felt the small, crowded room yawn open around him. The clumsy metal bookshelves filled with account ledgers and sales catalogs. The company calendar and wall clock. The framed photo of Angela and the kids.

"I think I told him to piss off, get away from me or else, you know."

"Or else what?"

"I'd file a report with Employee Relations. For the one thing, you know, the one thing they could nail him for."

"Interspecies harassment."

Hubert collapsed into his wide-back swivel chair. He closed his eyes and placed his hand on the cold, hissing intercom.

"And the scary thing, Stan? I think I meant it, too."

"I don't think it's because Harry's a wolf," Angela confessed to Muriel on their way home that night from the fund-raising committee. "I think it's more because he's a guy, and a middle management guy at that. Other guys, especially guys higher up the corporate ladder, make Hubie nervous; they always have. Anyway, Hubie has never been what you'd call a social individual. Not like your Harry."

Muriel lit her long, filtered menthol off the dashboard lighter and peered through her thwipping wipers at the foggy, dim-lit street ahead.

"I know there's nothing you can do, Angela. It just seems such a shame."

"I know, Muriel. I *know*."

Angela hated driving through the border regions, even in a car as large, luxurious, and well equipped as Muriel's SUV. Ever since the Cultural Intercession, it was the one part of town that hadn't changed, populated by the same bankrupt strip malls, triple-X-rated bookstores, and velour-curtained massage parlors.

"I keep thinking it'll blow over," Angela thought out loud, "and they'll get used to each other. Like you and me, Muriel; or even the kids. You think Hubie'd appreciate the open-minded ones like Harry who were so instrumental, you know. In creating so many new opportunities."

Muriel had yet to shift beyond first gear as they crawled through the close-packed urban streets, rocky with potholes, overturned trash cans and soggy, unraked leaves. Every few seconds, Muriel reactivated the door-lock mechanism. Just to make sure.

"It bothers Harry, that's all. And I can't pretend it doesn't," Muriel said. "You know, the way Hubie acts around us, those nervous little flinches of his. And the way he paces around until he's memorized every possible exit before he'll even sit in the same room as us. That night we had you over for dinner, Jesus. He made me so uncomfortable; even the kids noticed. And by the time we sat down to those veggieburgers I couldn't eat a thing, and then Hubie—"

"Please, Muriel. It's not like I don't remember."

"Please let me finish. And then the way Hubie got up and pretended he'd been beeped on his cell phone and took off like that, problem with the sales brochures or something, and knocking over his bowl on the floor he was in such a hurry to leave he didn't even look back he just—"

"*Watch out!*"

In that fractured moment it was as if some belated impulse had caught up with them. Muriel slammed on the brakes.

We've been here before, Angela thought mystically. Muriel and I, floating through space for eternities, finding our way home to this recurring moment, again and again.

There was a terrible, short-lived *thunk* and a brief glimpse of aborted momentum. Then a clutch of brightly adorned rags landed solidly in the street.

The large fat rat sat frozen in the electric white glare of the SUV's high beams and partially turned to regard them, glinty mouth agape.

"Oh, Jesus, Angela. I didn't see him. I really didn't."

The rat, clad in a hooded sweatshirt and latex jogging trunks, shook animation into his face and fingers. He got to his feet. He rubbed his furry forehead.

After a stunned moment, he exploded into words.

"What the *fuck* do you think you're doing?"

"Come on, Muriel. Let's get out of here."

The rat acquired a weird stature in the SUV's moonish emanations. He started toward them slowly, swinging his scraggly arms from side to side.

"You drive these boats through our neighborhoods like you *own* the place!"

Muriel looked over both shoulders while groping blindly for the clutch.

"Just back up, Muriel. Back up and get us out of here."

"You hear what I'm telling you? You fucking wolves and pigs think you own the place! Well, not in my book, sisters! Come on! Get outta that fucking car! Talk to me face to face!"

There was a backward lurch and kick from the clutch as the motor stalled and Muriel hit the ignition. The starter was grinding brokenly, like an obstructed blender.

"I really didn't see him," Muriel whispered as the engine finally caught and fired. Then, with two sweeps of the steering wheel, she backed into a driveway and took them swerving down the opposite side of the street. "I mean, why would I, he's acting like—"

"Come back here and show me your driver's license, you crazy bitches! You think you can just knock us down in the street and run away from your responsibilities?"

Angela watched the shrouded rat recede in the rearview mirror until distance and street engulfed him. Every few moments or so, the SUV hit an obstruction, lifted off the ground, and came down again with a smooth, well-engineered glide.

"Don't tell Harry," Muriel said. "He's been so worried about the office. I don't want him to start worrying about me and the kids, too."

But Angela couldn't hear her. All she could think about was what she was going to tell Hubie when she got home.

"You practically got us *killed*!" she shouted palely, shaking her red weskit at him like a hyperactive toreador. "We should have been watching the road and paying attention. But all we could think about was *you*, Hubert P. Armstrong! You and your petty, childish, and yes, Hubie, your *bigoted*, old-fashioned attitudes about wolves. Maybe you haven't quite noticed yet, Hubie, but this *is* the twenty-first century. Wolves don't exactly run in packs and howl at the moon any more than we root around in our own feces.

Animals change over time, Hubie. They adopt, adapt, improve. Otherwise the world wouldn't get any better, we wouldn't learn anything, we wouldn't grow up. Harry's sick over the way you treat him. And Muriel, and me— even *I'm* sick of the way you act. I mean, Muriel is like my only friend left since the Intercession, and I'm *proud* of the way I've opened our home to her and the kids. And I'm telling you, Hubert, if you're not proud of me, too, if you're not going to support me in showing a little animal decency to our new neighbors, then, then . . ."

Angela was running out of gas, issuing faint, grayish sputters from her thin, pink lips, like a dying outboard. Meanwhile, Hubert sat alone at the dining room table, staring ashamedly into his cardboard container of truffles in black bean sauce.

"I never meant to upset you, Angel," he said softly. "I just can't help the way I feel."

The red weskit fell from her hand to the floor, distinctly, like punctuation.

"Your feelings, Hubert, have nothing, they haven't got anything to do with, I mean—*my* feelings, Hubert, and *Muriel's* feelings . . ."

Hubert didn't feel capable of replying or moving a muscle. But then, somewhere deep inside himself, words gathered and cohered. Words that didn't have anything to do with him, or Angela, or even Harry.

He replaced the carton of Chinese food on the stain it had left on his white cotton napkin. Carton and stain— a perfect fit.

"I've thought long and hard about everybody's feelings, Angela. I really have. I went to work with Harry every day on the same bus for months. I watched him and the kids move in next door, attend block parties, and play with our kids in the yard. I never sneered at them or shouted insults, and when I saw those kids down the road throwing rocks at their car that day, remember. You remember what I did?"

"I remember, Hubert." Angela sat down in the crimson stuffed chair. Hubert often thought of it as the sad chair.

"I told them to go home, I'd call their parents, and they *went*, Angel. Look, I know my behavior hasn't been, well, exemplary, but I never meant to be rude, and I still keep wondering. Don't I have any rights in this matter? Don't my feelings count, too? I know I should look Harry in the eye and smile at Muriel and let the kids snap at my heels, but I just *can't* do it. It sends me into a panic. I can't even sleep anymore. And I just keep asking myself, maybe I'm wrong. Maybe wolves *have* changed, and maybe I *haven't* changed enough. But this daily corporate and social pressure they're exerting, it's just not fair. I thought freedom meant being free to think the wrong thing from time to time. But the sort of freedom you guys are talking? Well, I'm sorry. That doesn't feel like freedom at all."

Long after he tucked Angela into bed and kissed her good night, Hubert sat awake watching an old cop-buddy movie from his childhood. Entitled *Fatal Fire*, it featured exploding automobiles, collapsing skyscrapers, and two scowling, innately sentimental action stars who were constantly following one another into scenes of rapid-fire mayhem—a wolf who hated being partner to a pig, and a pig who hated being partner to a wolf. Hubert was surprised to find himself two beats ahead of the more memorable dialogue.

"Bite my pink butt, Furball!"

Or, "You know what I like best about pigs, short stuff? The gravy!"

It was where the Cultural Intercession had begun several years ago, just before the schools were merged and the suburbs desegregated. And to this day, it was where Hubert felt the Cultural Intercession should have ended.

Just before dawn, Hubert awoke on the sofa in a pale, crinkly moondust of Pringles. He heard the toilet flush upstairs and the soft, distant burbling of *Chick Chat* on Cissy's transistor radio. Which pup bands are your favorite, Allison from Maidenhead? Which pup stars? Have you entered our Become a Pup Star competition? Submit your photos now.

Hubert rubbed his puffy cheeks, went to the front window, and pried back the insulated curtains to see the glowing green lawns and dimming streetlights of Paradise Village Estates. A few early risers were already leaning rickety aluminum stepladders against rooftops, or washing their cars with sudsy water. Harry the Wolf, clad in his wife's billowy chiffon robe and a pair of tattered sweatpants, stood at the foot of his driveway, unsnapping the *Herald* and saying something to Sid Field across the street. Sid, the first pig to be booted upstairs to management, was all cheery and waving and come over for coffee.

Big surprise, Hubert mused.

Then he heard a whisper of padded slippers on the carpeted stairs. He turned.

"Morning, Daddy."

Cissy, adolescently blooming, was carrying a stuffed wolf absently under one armpit. A gift from Angela's mother, it had been well chewed and mauled over the years into a moppy clump.

"Morning, sweetheart. I'm glad you're up. Why don't I make us some pancakes, just you and me. Like old times."

Hubert folded the curtains closed. It felt like snuggling under a warm blanket. Mommy, piglets, hot water bottle, and me.

"Can't, Daddy. On a diet. *You* know."

"A *diet*? You've got to be kidding. My big, beautiful—"

It didn't sound like Cissy sighing. It sounded like the whole world.

"Please, Daddy. Let's not go over this again."

"How about juice then, and oh, it kind of depresses me to think about, but maybe we could share one of those protein bars you're always chomping."

"Done deal, Daddy. Can I play the radio?"

"Absolutely, princess. You listen to your *Chick Chat* and I'll get us breakfast."

Even before Hubert had filed the appropriate papers, he was called in by a submanagement team for what they called a "preliminary intervention."

"Sometimes employees can't resolve differences between themselves," Sid Field said, flanked by two middle-management wolves from Employee Relations. "These disagreements may be relatively insignificant at first. But left untreated, they grow exacerbated, and the infection spreads. Misunderstandings multiply; the organization suffers. As one of our senior sales specialists, Hubert, you must know the importance of keeping a happy camp. So please, before you file for arbitration, why not sit down with Harry and me and, say, another mediator of your choice, and let's see if we can settle this amicably. Maybe not as friends, but as compadres. We're all on the same team, Hubie. Whether we like it or not."

The wolves sat silently taking notes, sipping their limey sparkling water, and avoiding any exchange of eye contact that might betray a sense of accord.

"I didn't lose my temper and I didn't back down," Hubert told Stan later that afternoon at the company bar and grill. "Because that's what they're looking for, right? Either I wither in the gaze of those big wolfish grins—and I was shaking, boy, underneath my weskit I was sweating like a fool—or worse, maybe I start raving about a lupine monopoly, some secret conspiracy of Satanic carnivores yadda yadda, and then I'm lost. They'll dismiss me with a stroke of their pens. I never asked for this fight, Stan, but if they want to take me on, well. I will do everything they fear. Look them in the eyes. Stand my ground. And not do anything they can use against me in the court of public opinion. Your biggest enemy in a battle like this is yourself, Stan. It's not the other guy you should fear. It's always, always *you*."

"He didn't budge," Sid Field said in a late-night call from the office. "We did our best."

"I'm sure you did," Harry replied softly. He was sitting in the kitchen with his hot chocolate while Muriel cling-wrapped leftovers and pretended not to overhear.

"But something's come over Hubie. He's not his normal self."

"Thanks for trying," Harry said. Scum was forming on his milk. He hated when that happened. "I know you need to get home."

Sid carried on, compelled by some inner momentum. "It's like Hubie never really existed before you guys moved in, and I don't mean just you and Muriel. I mean you and the other wolves. Back during the, you know."

"The Intercession," Harry said.

Muriel looked up from her long-secured pasta and tofu. "I'll go check on the kids," she said after a moment.

Harry had waited to be left alone all day.

"I guess we'll go through with it and hope for the best," Harry said finally, after the kitchen door closed.

"I mean it, Harry. Hubie was always the quietest guy I knew, no rough edges, happy as a clam. Did whatever needed to be done, couldn't give a crap about politics and upmanship and so forth. But then you guys started moving in, and it sort of defined him somehow. He became a more visible entity. He never use to be the sort of pig to give anybody any trouble, and now he's the last pig to give an inch."

Harry felt conscripted somehow. It was as if this thin telephone line, relayed across space by satellite beams and high-fiber optics, articulated him with a scheme of other thoughts, other interests.

"I guess I'll see you tomorrow, then."

"Absolutely, Harry. The boss thought I should maintain a presence because, well—I guess that's obvious."

"And the others?"

"That's what I wanted to ask—"

Harry would put an end to this right now.

"Bring in someone from another office. Someone I haven't worked with. Someone with no particular, you know, interests."

It took all the wind out of Sid's sails.

"Oh," Sid said. "So that's how you want it."

"That's how I want it," Harry said, and took his hot chocolate to the sink, where he lifted off the lid of steamed cream with a fork and laid it in the trash can. "Completely on the up and up. Let's give Hubie his day in court and settle things once and for all. When this is over, I want it to be *really* over; I don't want to see any appeals or reapplications. When this is over, let's close the book on this sorry episode and move on."

"I just want to say I don't hold anything personal against Harry the Wolf," Hubert began. "He's a decent administrator, a dependable neighbor, and hell, I almost said a good friend, but that's why I'm here, isn't it? To say that Harry and I will *never* become friends. We will never become *friendly*. Even if I accept all the economic and social reforms of the past few years, those are external changes we're talking about. Matters of public policy, demographics, procedure, what have you. But what Harry can't understand—what none of you seem to understand—is that I can't change who I am inside. That's my nature, my inherent—I don't know. My basic cellular stuff. I'm not saying it's right to be anxious or, oh, hell, let me come out and say it. I'm not saying it's right to *hate* wolves. And I *do*, I really *hate* them. I loathe their pinkish eyes and toothy grins and those paws of theirs; I don't care how much they pay for their manicures. Those rough, chitinous paws patting me on the back at a company mixer, it's like they're checking me out, right? My juice, my mass, how nice I'll fit on the plate. The way I've been made to feel by Harry and the rest of you—even by my fellow pigs like Sid there—isn't fair. It interferes with my work, my family, my everything. I don't want to bring these charges against Harry, I don't want to file a non-molestation order, but if I have to, believe me, I will. But first I need to air my grievances at an official hearing of my peers, even if most of you *are* wolves. And make a suggestion."

Hubert already had their attention. But now, as he

glanced around the room and made eye contact with every individual at the table, he let them know it.

"Clearly, you guys think I do a good job in sales. Well, let me get on with it. Stop trying to intimidate me into attending bispecies company functions, and let me set up my own office. We're talking about expansion, anyway. Let me run my Sales Department in a separate building where I'm not surrounded by all these hostile scents and glances. I know it's segregation. I know it's a break with reform. And I know I'll still be going home each night to find wolves on my sidewalks, wolves in my shopping centers and coffee shops. But if I have one place to go every day in which to achieve some semblance of peace and sanctity, well. I'll do a better job. I'll sell more goddamn veggie pies. And that's what this is all about, right? Selling more veggie pies. Opening up the market and bringing down costs and increasing revenue. Well, I can do that, but not the way Harry wants it. Not as, you know—not as *friends*."

Hubert looked directly at Harry with neither fear nor condemnation. It was the strongest, most basic animal emotion Hubert had felt for anybody in a long time.

Hubert was *sorry*.

"And I really *am* sorry, Harry. I'm truly *sorry* for how I feel. But I can't work with you in the same office, breathing down my neck, hankering after my affection. I just can't feel friendship for you, guy. And I never will."

Harry was "promoted" to Pensions, while Hubert was granted two and a half of his three wishes. He was allowed to transfer his entirely porcine sales force to a newish set of trailer blocks out in the old, and largely abandoned, industrial park; he was relieved from attending all company functions, even the Christmas mixer; and while his office was visited every alternate Wednesday by a lupine auditor from Central, it was generally acknowledged that Hubert's absences from these meetings required little if any explanation from his administrative assistant, Stacey.

"Hubert wanted me to let you know he's out visiting some of the local shops as part of his loyalties campaign. But everything you need's on his desk."

There were still occasional awkward suburban mishaps, when the wrong sorts of individuals encountered one another in the frozen-food aisles of supermarkets, or while driving through the popular new Tofu-Delight down at Lakeshore.

"Hey there, Harry! How're they hanging—oops, sorry, Muriel. Doing your nongender-specific shopping?"

"Oh, hi, Hubie. Excuse me, let me just reach that jumbo carton of wild-grain brown rice off the top shelf—"

"Here you go, Harry. You're looking a little creaky."

"Thanks, yeah. My back's acting up."

"How are things upstairs with the big boys? I hear you're knocking 'em dead in Pensions."

"Yes, well, nice seeing you, Hubert. I'll just get out of your way now—"

"No problem, Harry. Oh—and Muriel! Did Angel give you a call? She wanted you to know—"

"That's fine, Hubert. Everything's straight for tomorrow. You take care of yourself, okay?"

It was funny, Hubert thought, how all the fear and haste just melted away once you didn't have to see them anymore, didn't have to look them in the eye. Suddenly everything was easier. The air pressure shifted. You could walk in the open air and be free.

"You'll never believe who I ran into at A&P."

"Muriel told me. Could you please pass the butter, Hubie?"

Cissy was on the kitchen phone talking about some boy. He was cute. He had his own car.

"He didn't look like his old self, if you know what I mean."

"Harry takes his responsibilities pretty seriously, Hubie. As an administrator, as a neighbor. He doesn't just—"

"Doesn't just what?"

"Let's leave it, Hubie. How do you feel about dessert?"

"Doesn't just *what*, Angel?"

Angela had adopted Cissy's diet about the same time Cissy dropped it. The Dr. Atkins all-protein diet: rice and fish and this milky, brothlike substance three times per day. As a result, she always seemed in a terrible temper.

"He doesn't just look at account ledgers, Hubie." She was taking up the plates and glasses. "He doesn't just keep track of the bottom line. When you have, you know, ideals about your world, Hubie, and about how you want to live your life, well, you put a lot of pressure on yourself. You're not just trying to, you know, cover your bottom."

Hubert was left at the dining room table with his half-finished glass of Beaujolais nouveau. It felt like disappearing into three weeks ago. That was how long he had been waiting for Angela to tell him exactly what she just said.

Cissy was still speaking breathlessly into the cordless. "I think he does like me, Ginger. That's what I'm trying to tell you. His friend, you know his friend, Kevin? Kevin told me he likes me. The next time I see him at band practice, I haven't got any idea what to say!"

It was so nice to be young, Hubert thought. To get so excited about things, as if this were the very first time they had happened to anybody.

"I never meant to hurt Harry, or Muriel, or you," Hubert whispered as Angela began clattering dishes in the sink. "I just needed to make it through the day. I needed to wake up in the morning with the belief, however mistaken, that my life was starting over again. And that I wasn't responsible to anybody in the entire world but myself."

He loped breathlessly through the hoary woods, pursued by plump pink pigs bearing shotguns and torches. Expressionistic shadows leaped past. He smelled roast meat in the timbery air.

"Let's *get* him! Let's get Harry the Wolf!"

. . . and awoke on the living room sofa, dripping sweat from his furry nostrils. He was clutching his wife's chiffon bathrobe for a blanket. When he sat up, a half-empty fifth of Gordon's gin greeted him from the coffee table.

Harry rubbed his cheek absently with the sash of Muriel's bathrobe. It was funny the things you found comforting when you grew up. In Harry's case, it was the random stroke of corrugated chiffon.

He looked at the clock on the mantelpiece. It was nearly 10:00 AM.

"I've already called the office and told them you won't be in." Muriel's words still circulated in the motley darkness, struck through by several convening blades of sunlight from the faultily hung blackout curtains. "Try to have a decent breakfast, will you? I left muesli on the table and hard-boiled eggs. I'm not going to kiss you—I just put on makeup. But I love you, Harry the Wolf. Try to feel better. I might not always show it, but I love you very much."

Something like compassion accompanied her words. But not nearly as much compassion as yesterday. Or the day before that.

"I love you, too," Harry muttered dryly in the empty sitting room. He topped up his cut crystal glass (a wedding gift from Muriel's sister) and wet his whistle. What a funny expression, Harry thought. Wetting my whistle.

It probably has something to do with being a wolf.

Then he activated the flat-screen TV with his remote control.

"In other business news today, sales figures at International Wolf and Pig have reported higher profit-taking than expected, and that's led to fierce trading on the Nikei, which sent the Euro plummeting—"

There was a time when Harry knew what they were talking about on Bloomberg Television. But that was a long time ago.

"For years I believed in things," Harry had told his therapist at the company clinic only two afternoons back. "I believed in making the world better for our children. I believed in liberal social reforms, conservative foreign policy, paying off the national debt, and anything to do with child protection or gun control. But most of all, I believed that the government didn't solve your problems; only *you* did. So when I saw what segregation was doing to our children, our neighborhoods, and our schools, I went to the CEO. I started talking up reforms with the board. I reminded them all, them and the stockholders, that a company was about more than the bottom line. It was about ethical business practices. It was about diversification across the mainstream community. It was about opening new zones to enterprise, profit, and control. Let's face it, we had the wolf market sewn up; we were growing lazy and unprofitable. You can't build a better society by recycling the same capital over and over again. You need new ideas. You need new blood."

Harry replaced his empty glass on the coffee table. He looked at the fifth of Gordon's gin.

It was too early for Gordon's gin.

He was just picking up the bottle when the doorbell rang.

"I remember driving by Pig Paradise with my dad when I was just a kid," Harry said out loud as he tied the sash of Muriel's bathrobe loosely around his waist. "It was the first upscale planned community for their species; my dad and his partners built it from nothing but a vast dead stretch of mud, half-chewed corncobs, and pig feces. The tidy little streets and green spaces. The local shops and buses. It was like they were being given everything we wolves had taken for granted over the years, and you wouldn't believe how soon they got used to it. They took it for granted in no time."

The doorbell buzzed and buzzed.

"I'm coming," Harry said. "I'm *coming*!" And opened the door.

The little rat was propped up on a pair of wooden crutches, like one of those automatons that emerged every year from the Christmas clock outside Army & Navy. He wore a hooded sweatshirt and lots of glittery urban gear.

"Harry the Wolf," he said, as if they had known one another all their lives. "You own that bloody Range Rover in the driveway. And you got a wife, man. A wife with no respect for the law."

It was as if a switch had been thrown in a remote part of Harry's brain. He had been waiting for this particular switch to be thrown for a long, long time.

"I'm sorry, I can't help you right now. Here."

Harry sloshed some petty change from a bowl on the side table. He held it out like a stale bouquet.

"Just move along, will you? I don't want to call the cops."

"*You* don't wanta call the cops. *You* don't wanta call the cops on *me*? A normal, everyday working guy who gets run down in the middle of the street by some lupine tart in an urban assault vehicle. Of all the goddamn nerve . . ."

Harry felt as if he had been gripped by a conveyor belt in a department store, carrying him into higher realms of experience. Hardware, kitchen appliances, children's wear, bedding.

"I haven't worked in three weeks 'cause of you and your fancy white-collar families using my neighborhood like a racetrack 'cause you're so fucking scared you'll get carjacked or some bloody thing as if you wolves and pigs are any better with your fancy houses and department stores and big posh Thai restaurants with the signs outside, right? No Rats Allowed. No Rats Allowed. As if we'd ever spend two cents on that designer crap you feed yourselves and then I'm walking home, right, I'm minding my own business in my own neighborhood like I'm supposed to and your bloody wife, Mac, your bloody wife and her bloody pig girlfriend . . ."

It was neither fear nor hunger, Harry thought, as his entire body contracted into itself. It was more like contentment, a small kernel of himself he hadn't visited in a long time. Just to be yourself and know yourself, he thought. Like they're always telling you on TV.

". . . and all I wanta know, right, is who pays for what I lost, that's all *I* wanta know," the beady little rat continued, poking his little forepaw at Harry's chest, poke poke poke. "You with your big fancy house and cars and jobs in the city and your pension plans and medical. Who pays for what we lose, right? I think it's gonna be you, Harry the Wolf! I think it's gonna have to be *you!*"

• • •

Hubert arrived home that night to find emergency vehicles in his driveway, swirling with half-tone urgency and light. Across the street, Harry's house was cordoned off by big, bluff coppers waving illuminated batons. A precinct captain was taking Angela's statement in the middle of Hubert's front yard.

"We came home," Angela stated haltingly, as if she were delivering a series of unfinished aphorisms. "Muriel was already upset. Harry's been acting funny lately, and I don't want to say anything that will . . . Oh, Hubert! I'm so glad you're home!"

"What's this all about?" Hubert asked woodenly. He felt as if he were dissembling. "Angel, you're ghost-white. Let's go in and sit down."

"I just need to ask a few more questions," the police captain said.

"Come on, Angel. Let's get inside, and this captain, I'm sorry . . ."

"Captain Pierce."

"Captain Pierce can ask his questions when you're ready. And if you're not ready, Captain Pierce can come back tomorrow. How does that sound to you, Captain Pierce?"

When they went inside they found photographers and news reporters sitting on all the chairs and open spaces, scribbling into notepads and eating prepackaged sandwiches. Oblivious to everyone around her, Cissy was on the phone to her best friend, Juanita.

"It was like *The Exorcist* in there, I swear," Cissy emoted. She had never looked so flushed and hectic before. "Or some Hong Kong action flick. Blood all over the walls and ceiling and Harry—you know Harry, don't you, as in Rupert's dad?—Harry collapsed in the middle of it all like a big, furry rag doll. Police and ambulances and reporters everywhere but there was nothing anybody could do, and if you ask me, why bother? Yes, a rat, Juanita, a big smelly germ-ridden *rat* with those big pointy teeth they get, you know? Like they're chewing on wood all day, tunneling through walls and sewer pipes. I mean, I'm sure it was just instinct, you know? Harry couldn't help himself and, oh, no."

Something flashed behind Cissy's eyes that wasn't reflection.

"I think I'm going to be sick."

And right there, in the liminal spaces dividing Hubert's sitting room from his kitchen, Cissy was.

She was sick all over the floor.

It was a fair trial, during which nobody paid much attention to either the street protesters, or to the "investigative" news journalists, who made such a public display of themselves.

"Harry! Could we have a word? Harry the Wolf!"

"I'm sorry, please make way. My client wishes to make no comments at this time."

"Harry, please! We think the public has a right to know!"

"Justice now! Justice now! Justice now!"

"My client will be filing his pleas later this morning and then we'll let the jury decide. If Harry has any comments, we've advised that he make them *after* the trial."

"Harry! Harry! Do you remember me? Consuela Rodriguez from Public Access; we met during those housing demos you organized during the early eighties. What do you say, Harry, to all those wolves and pigs who criticized your liberal reform initiatives back then, arguing that pigs and wolves could never come together in civic harmony? There are a lot of people here today who think that this is *exactly*—"

"*Justice now! Justice now!*"

"*Three species—one law!*"

"*One law now! One law now!*"

"—just the sort of irrepressible violence that's bound to occur whenever, you know—"

"Please, Ms. Rodriguez, please make way for—"

"No, I want to answer that."

Seated at home on his well-molded settee, Hubert suffered a fizzy cellular lapse and took a long lonely sip of his Bovril. This was what you didn't expect from TV anymore—the lonely, accidental flux of real life.

"Please, Harry, I don't think this is—"

"I said I want to answer that."

Harry was wearing a three-piece hound's tooth suit and a bland pastel tie.

"I just want to say to Consuela, and to the people sitting at home . . ."

Hubert blinked.

". . . that this has nothing to do with the, the ideals I cherish of a free and equal society. It has, has nothing to do, nothing at all . . ."

Harry's voice trailed off. Even the protesters faded slowly in the background, as if someone were turning down the volume or adjusting the tone.

"I guess what I'm trying, trying to say—"

"Come on, Harry. Let's go in and sit down."

It was the touch of the lawyer's hand on his well-tailored shoulder that did it. In a slow, autonomic flinch, Harry turned his head and started to cry, big wolfish tears coursing down his graying furry nose like a streaky rain falling nowhere in the world but here.

"That's all my client has to say right now. Please, please make room for us, will you? We'll be making a full statement once the trial is concluded."

When the six-month sentence for involuntary manslaughter was handed down (and summarily suspended), there were a few hot nights in the urban wasteland, but nobody paid much attention to *them*. Rats setting fire to their own streets and trash cans. Rats hurling rocks at police vans and fire trucks. Rats shrieking and screaming to be recognized as equals when they couldn't comport themselves any better than who they really were. Dirty, stinking, smelly, low-life little vermin. Nobody could help creatures like that. Especially if they couldn't help themselves.

"Let them piss on their own front stoops for all I care," Sid told Hubert one morning in the street. Their morning papers had landed side by side in the gutter (Sid's neoconservative *Tribune* and Hubie's neoliberal *Times*), so mutually enshrouded by leaves, candy wrappers, and road gunk that it was hard to tell them apart. "Anyway," Sid concluded, allowing his gaze to drift coolly to the neighboring driveway, "at least now the whole damn mess is over and we can get back to work. Did I tell you, Hubie? I've requested a transfer to your all-porcine building, so maybe we can start grabbing lunch again. I know this place in the area, great swill, great grog, and no you-know-whos. We've grown apart over the past year, Hubie. Maybe we could mend fences and be friends."

But Hubert felt increasingly disconsolate and unresolved. After the trial, Harry, Muriel, and the kids left town for a two-month "recuperation," and Hubert volunteered (through the intermediary of Angela) to water their lawn, collect the mail, and pay any urgent bills with a set of signed blank checks Muriel left on the kitchen table. Hubert hadn't seen Harry face to face since that awkward afternoon at the local Safeway. Yet every moment he spent in the large, well-appointed ranch-style home, he could hear Harry everywhere.

"I always wanted those orange tiles in the bathroom," Harry's voice intoned whenever Hubert entered the downstairs bathroom. "I saw them in an architectural brochure and *had* to have them. The first time we saw this house, we fell in love. All that space in the yard, Hubert. Space where the kids could run and play. Space for thinking, and being, and shaping yourself. We didn't have to worry about the traffic, or the noise, or the pollution, or the—you know. The other temptations pups face every day in the overcrowded, hungry cities. I really love this house, Hubert, and I'm glad you're finally taking a look around. See, here's my workshop in the basement. And the varnished oak paneling in the den? I installed that myself. I guess this is what makes us different from the beasts of the jungle. The effort to make our homes permanent and everlasting. A place for our kids to grow up. A place that provides comfort, and sanctity, and surplus for our friends, our loved ones, and ourselves."

Some days, Hubert would sit in Harry's favorite chair in the living room and listen to jazz CDS on the stereo, sipping Cockburn's ruby port from a brandy snifter and waiting for the phone to ring.

"Hubie? What are you doing over there?"

"Nothing, Angel. Just closing up."

"You've been hours, honey. How long does it take to pay an electric bill and feed the hamster?"

Hubert replaced his brandy snifter on the mahogany coffee table. He had almost forgotten the hamster.

"I was just leaving."

"I know they said make yourself at home, Hubie. But I don't feel right about you spending so much time there. Also, I got a card from Muriel this morning. You ought to know."

Hubert felt the stomach drop out of him and sat back down in Harry's favorite stuffed chair. It had to happen eventually. He certainly deserved it.

"What's that, Angel?"

"The realtors are coming tomorrow and putting up a sign. Does that make you happy—to get what you always wanted? Harry's taking early retirement and they're moving to the country. That way, they can finally be closer to Muriel's folks."

Several months later, after moving vans deposited a new family into what Hubert would always think of as Harry's house, Hubert donned his best red weskit and pinkest bow tie and drove downtown in the new minivan. It was a windy, weather-racked autumn day. Leaves swirled in gutters, and frost gathered on windows.

It was the only house in this part of town without a broken car in the driveway.

The buzzer didn't work; but the cracked iron knocker did.

"Who is it?"

A chain lock permitted the door to open a few inches. A gleamless black eye peered from inside the dark, burrowy cottage.

"My name's Hubert. I work at Mama O'Brian's All-Veggie Pies and I'm sorry to bother you. Could I come in?"

"What yuh need tuh come in for? I can see yuh just fine."

"I know, but I just thought—"

"Yer a pig."

"I sure am."

"Yuh from the bank or yuh from the council?"

"Neither, ma'am. It's just that I heard about your loss—"

"My loss? Yer not another newspaper creep, are yuh?"

"I work in Regional Sales and we've just begun this new program, see. It's called Feed the World, and while I know that's biting off more than we can chew, no joke intended—"

"What're those boxes under yer arms?"

A black, rubbery snout replaced the black eyeball, snuffling intently.

"At Mama O'Brian's, we take pride in our pies—that's one of our mottoes—so when there's a flaw, it might be the slightest little fault in the crust, or the aluminum pie pan might get bumped or misshapen—"

The nose slowly withdrew. It had smelled everything it needed to know.

"I'm not signin' nothin'."

"I wouldn't ask you to."

"Yuh just want tuh give me pies?"

"That's all I want to do and, you know. When these pies are finished I can give you my work number, or better yet . . ."

Hubert bent over and placed two large cartons on the weedy stoop. Then he removed the business card from his vest pocket and scribbled something on its back.

"My home number. I live right up the road and maybe, well, we've got this nice, big yard where your kids might like to play sometime. It's called—"

"I know what it's called."

"It's called, well, these days it's just called Paradise. That's how I think of it, anyway. The most beautiful place you're capable of imagining. The reward you get for being good, and for doing good things the best way you know how."

It was the only truth Hubert still knew.

And it continued resounding in his mouth as he heard the steel latch lift and watched the small door open.

Acknowledgments

The author is grateful to the following publications and their editors:

Triquarterly: "Penguins for Lunch"
Buzz Magazine: "Men and Women in Love"
The Printer's Devil: "Heaven Sent"
The Magazine of Fantasy and Science Fiction: "Angry Duck," "Dazzle Redux," "Dazzle's Inferno," "Doggy Love," and "The Devil Disinvests"; an earlier version of "The Devil Disinvests" appeared in *Swissair Gazette*
Off Limits (edited by Ellen Datlow): "Queen of the Apocalypse"
In Dreams (edited by Kim Newman and Paul McAuley): "The Reflection Once Removed"
The Denver Quarterly: "Big Paradise"
"The Anti-Santa," illustrated by Jack Bradfield, was originally issued as a signed, limited edition by Beccon Publications, 2002; it was reprinted in *The Idler*.
Black Heart, Ivory Bones (edited by Ellen Datlow and Terri Windling): "Goldilocks Tells All"

Additional thanks to my editor, Nate Knaebel, at Carroll & Graf for all of his help.

This book would not have been possible without the gracious support of the University of Connecticut.